I'm a Therapist, and My Patient is A Vegan Terrorist

6 Deadly Social Media Influencers

Dr. Harper

This is a work of fiction.

Names, characters, businesses, places, events, locales, and incidents are either the products of the author's imagination or used in a fictitious manner.

Any resemblance to actual persons, living or dead, or actual events is purely coincidental.

DEDICATION

Thank you, for following Dr. Harper & Noah to the end.

THE INFLUENCER FILES

Sometimes I wonder...

Would I be happier if I made a different choice?

PATIENT FILES

Our First Date

"All aboard the S.S. Harper!"

I hurried over to Doc and pulled him into a tight hug. He returned the embrace, but kept his face to the side of mine. I wondered if that was intentional. Even though we already kissed a long time ago, we hadn't kissed since he agreed to go on a date with me, so it sort of felt like we needed to go through the first kiss awkwardness all over again.

Or maybe I was overthinking things, as usual.

"How have you been, Noah?" Doc pulled away slightly.

"Good — I mean, great!" I said, taking his bags. "Well, great *now*! How was your trip?"

"A lot easier after the exoneration," he said. "Thanks for that, by the way."

Between Zach's investigations of the pedophile ring and the cult, there was so much public outcry that Doc was quickly exonerated and able to come out of hiding.

"Looks like they're ready for us!" I said, pointing at Kierra and Zach on the bow of the boat. They waved at us.

Doc waved back, although I could tell his friendliness was reserved only for Zach.

As we made our way onto the ship, several crew

members took his bags and directed us toward the front.

Doc raised his eyebrows as Zach came over and clapped him on the back.

"How the hell did you guys afford all this?" Doc asked.

"My books are selling like crazy," said Zach. "And they wouldn't really exist without you, so I figured this was the least I could do."

Zach stepped back, leaving Kierra as the next logical person to greet.

Doc stared at her for a few moments and cleared his throat.

"Hi," he said stiffly.

"Oh my gosh!" she said, fanning her face with her hands. "This is my first time meeting a celebrity."

He gave her a dirty look, although she wasn't exactly wrong. Ever since the exoneration, Doc's name had been plastered online and all over the news. His presence was now one of the biggest "attractions" at the festival.

"Just don't let it get to that big head of yours," she said with a wink. "Can't fit too much more in there before it pops."

"Annnd the bitch is back..." Doc grumbled.

"We're like the dream team!" I interrupted them, trying to prevent a fight. Sometimes I talk a lot, because it distracts people from getting angry. My therapist told me not to worry about other peoples' conflicts, but I really wanted this evening to be perfect.

Doc screwed up his face. "How are we the dream team?"

"Well, you're the hero of course," I said hurriedly.

Kierra made a retching sound.

"And Kierra — she keeps your ego in check..."

Doc rolled his eyes as she nodded proudly.

"I'm the comic relief, obviously," I continued. "And I guess Zach is sort of our dad. You know, the only real adult around here."

"I'll take it," said Zach.

"Hey, I'm an adult!" Doc protested.

"Yeah..." muttered Kierra. "A psychotic man-baby who kidnaps anyone that disagrees with him."

Doc's face went red. "I am not a man-baby—"

"See? It's perfect!" I stepped between them with a nervous smile. "So, is everyone excited for the big trip?"

Kierra and Doc crossed their arms.

To my relief, Zach spoke up before they could continue arguing.

"Kierra, I need some help down in the kitchen."

I gave him a thankful look and he winked as they disappeared down below.

"Noah, why is Kierra here?" asked Doc. "You *have* to know she's unchanged."

"Let's talk about that later!" I said. There actually was a big reason I trusted her, but she made me promise not to tell him. "I want to show you something on the main deck."

He eyed me curiously and nodded.

When we got to the deck on the front of the boat, everything was exactly as I had left it. A hot air balloon, fully inflated, just like the one from our stories. Inside the basket, a table and two chairs set for dinner.

I turned to Doc, eager to see his reaction, but he didn't say anything.

"It's not fully functional," I said. "I asked if we could float to the island over the ocean, but apparently that's not safe — or humanly possible. So I figured we could make our own!"

Doc turned to me. "You did all of this?"

"I did!" I said. "I wanted our first date to be special."

He raised his eyebrows. "Date?"

"Well, yeah!" I felt my heart drop. "Wait, you wanted to go on a date, right?"

"Yes!" he said quickly. "I did — I do. Sorry, I just didn't know it would be this... nice. I would have worn a collared shirt."

He gave me an encouraging smile, and I relaxed.

"Okay, phew! Because I've planned a surprise date for every night on the island," I said, monitoring his reactions carefully. "Unless you don't want to date me anymore — which is totally fine too. I just mean, there's no pressure to keep going on dates if you don't like this one."

Okay, maybe I wasn't totally relaxed.

"Noah, I love it," he said. "Let's sit down."

We stepped into the balloon's basket and took a seat at the table.

As the boat took off from shore, the personal chef brought us dish after dish (all of Doc's favorite foods) until we couldn't eat another bite.

It was exactly as I imagined.

As we ate, we talked about everything. I learned more about what he went through in prison, and he asked me all about my time with Kierra. I tried not to share too many details that would upset him. And honestly, it wasn't that bad anyway.

"And you weren't hurt?" he asked for the third time. "Like, physically or emotionally?"

"No!" I said. "I promise. I actually spent most of the time working on my seven key plan."

He tilted his head. "Your seven key... what?"

"Oh, I forgot to tell you!" I reached into my pocket. "I've been working on a project to help people who struggle with feeling happy — the way I felt before you helped me. Even though I'm not a therapist, I just wanted to help others like you did for me."

"That's great," he said. "Like a book or something?"

"I don't know," I said, scanning through my notebook. "I haven't figured that part out yet. I'd like to make it free so anyone can use it. But I have to finish it first!"

"Am I allowed to ask what the seven keys are?"

"Hmmm..." I paused. "I wasn't planning on sharing it until I finished, but I guess I can give you one today!"

He nodded eagerly. "And then another one for each of our other dates?"

I did my best to conceal a huge smile. He had no idea how much that put me at ease — or, I don't know — maybe he did.

"Okay!" I said. "Well, the first key is nonjudgmental self-awareness. Like, we can't do any of the other keys until we're aware of our thought patterns — both positive and negative. I never even realized how mean I was to myself until you helped me notice it."

"I like it already," said Doc. "But Noah, you figured that out on your own. And honestly, you're probably better at it than I am."

With every word he spoke, I realized how much I had missed him.

He was so thoughtful and so... good. I know a lot of people are confused about where Doc stands — morally, I mean. But to me, it has never been a question.

We continued talking about the first key for a while, including some of the strategies I had come up with for implementing it. I kept expecting him to remind me that I wasn't a therapist — that I had no psychological credentials.

But he never did.

Instead, he listened with such genuine interest, asking question after question, until I completely lost track of time. Before we knew it, the shore was far out of sight and the sun was starting to set over the endless ocean.

As the sky turned orange and pink, we stood up and stepped out of the balloon, making our way to the railing at the front of the boat.

The views were endless, and the waves crashed all around us.

"Do you think something bad is actually going to happen?" I eventually broke the silence. "At the festival, I mean."

Doc shook his head. "Honestly, I don't know. The security at this thing is supposed to be airtight. I'm not sure how anyone could get past it. But Zach is... I don't know. I've never seen him like this. He wouldn't have asked us to come unless he was really worried."

I leaned in closer to him. "So what do you think it will be?"

"What do you mean?"

"Like if there really is a bad guy — or girl," I said. "What's it going to be? Some sort of shooting? A bomb? Another cult?"

He laughed. "If the stabby sisters are on this island, we're turning the boat around."

I laughed too.

We stood there together for a while, looking out over the starry sea. I kept glancing sideways at Doc to see if he was glancing back — to see if he was anticipating the same kiss that I was anticipating.

But instead, he seemed to be focused intently ahead of us. On the island we couldn't see yet.

We didn't kiss that night, but when it got a bit chillier, he put his arm around me and I felt my heart soar into the night sky.

"We're going to regret this, aren't we, Noah?"

I laughed nervously.

I wasn't quite sure if he was talking about the festival — or us.

Vegan Terrorist

Vegan Terrorist

PART ONE

"HOW DO YOU SPOT A VEGAN? THEY'LL TELL YOU HAHAHAHAHAHAHAHA!"

My eyes went wide as I watched the livestream unfold before me.

A human — crudely dressed as a chicken — was screaming at a young blonde woman on a leash.

"PETA. ACRONYM FOR PEOPLE EATING TASTY ANIMALS HAHAHAHAHAHAHAHA!"

The Chicken laughed maniacally, spitting blood all over the woman's face. It wasn't a real laugh. It was an angry, derisive laugh. And as if that wasn't bizarre enough, there was also a staticky version of *The Chicken Dance* was playing in the background.

I don't wanna be a chicken... I don't wanna be a duck... So I shake my butt!

The Chicken turned to the camera and tilted its head. It seemed to be wearing a standard Halloween chicken costume, googly-eyed glasses, bleached red hair, and crusty yellow face paint. It slowly broke into a smile, revealing a set of blood-stained teeth.

"Hey there, mother-cluckers."

The leashed woman at its feet let out a whimper. The Chicken whooped with glee and electrocuted her with some sort of cattle prod.

"FOR EVERY BURGER YOU DON'T EAT, I'LL EAT

TWO HAHAHAHAHAHAHAHA!"

The woman shrieked and writhed on the ground as The Chicken danced around her body, mimicking her cries.

I shut the laptop, unable to watch any more.

"What the fuck is this?" I breathed.

"We were hoping you could tell us," said Zach. "It's streaming live, from this island."

"And the woman? Do we know who she is?"

"Maggie Greenberg," said Zach, flipping through his notes. "A popular young conservative activist at the festival. Here's her Twitter profile: *Proud heterosexual. It's okay to be white. Collector of liberal tears. I don't give a fuck about your feelings.*"

He showed me a picture of an attractive woman posing by a Christmas tree with a rifle in each hand.

"What about the... Chicken?" I asked. "Any ideas who that might be?"

"Nothing." Zach shook his head. "So far, they're just repeating vegan-mocking Tweets from Maggie's account. They appear to be using some sort of voice scrambler. We can't even tell if it's male or female."

"So we have nothing."

"Well..." said Zach. "We have — we have a vegan."

I raised my eyebrows. "You have a *vegan?*"

"There's a vegan influencer here at the festival," said Zach. "We can't find him on the flight manifest and we can't dig up anything about him."

"Okay, then what do you need a therapist for? Shouldn't security be questioning him?"

"They *have*, Elliot," said Zach. "He's proven a bit... difficult to communicate with."

"What do you mean?" I asked.

"Please, just sit down with him," said Zach. "See what you can find out."

I nodded reluctantly, and Zach stood up to bring in the patient.

A young man walked through the door. He was overweight with a scraggly half-beard, wearing a frumpy old sweater and a pair of light brown corduroys.

"Shawn, I'd like to introduce you to Dr. Harper."

Shawn approached me, but he did not greet me or extend his hand. Instead, he gazed directly into my eyes for an uncomfortably long time.

"Elliot," said Zach. "This is Shawn. Shawn has taken a vow of silence, in solidarity with factory farm animals. He rose to internet fame by streaming his own emotional reactions to animal abuse videos — all without speaking a word."

"He doesn't speak?" I hissed at Zach. "That's kind of... a big part of therapy."

"He's been streaming his reactions to Maggie's abuse," Zach whispered back. "I'm worried that he seems to be showing less concern for a human being than a cow."

I sighed. "Okay. I'll see what I can do. But security needs to find that girl before this gets any worse."

"They're working it," he said quickly. "Thanks, Elliot."

Zach headed for the door, leaving me alone with Shawn and his weird eye contact.

There was nothing special about his gaze or expression. It wasn't positive or negative, happy or sad. It was just neutral — like an observer. I couldn't imagine why that would be attracting thousands of views on YouTube.

"Alright, Shawn." I broke his gaze and took a seat. "I understand that you're doing this silent protest thing, but there's a girl in serious danger out there. If there's something you know that could help, you need to tell the security team."

Shawn sat down too, and kept his eyes on mine.

I thought back in my life to the patients who insisted on inappropriate eye contact. Usually it was some sort of power play, personality disorder, or judgmental bullshit. But this didn't seem like any of those things. He genuinely just seemed to be... watching.

Zach of all people should have known that I didn't have the patience for this.

"Listen," I said, opening up my laptop. "There's just not enough time for this, so if you're going to watch something, let's watch the stream."

The video resumed to real-time, zooming in as The Chicken held up a piece of paper with a checklist:

1. *Debeaking*

2. *Forced—*

Before I could read the rest, the shaky camera jumped up and focused on The Chicken's face.

"Debeaking is... just about what it sounds like." The Chicken licked its lips. "Cutting off the beak, usually of a baby chick. That way, they don't cause any trouble when they're stuffed into a shit-filled cage as they await their death. As you can imagine, slicing off a part of your face tends to be a bit painful. Blisters in the mouth, nasty burns, sometimes the blade catches your tongue too."

The Chicken looked down at Maggie, who was still whimpering on the ground.

The Chicken knelt down next to her and tilted its head.

"It's all so FUNNY, isn't it, Maggie? Isn't it FUNNY when a baby bird has its face mutilated?"

Maggie shook her head and cried as *The Chicken Dance* reached crescendo.

I don't wanna be a chicken... I don't wanna be a duck... So I shake my butt!

"Yes, it's so FUNNY!" The Chicken reached down and stuck its hands into Maggie's mouth, forcing her jaw up and down in a strained laughing motion. "HAH HAH HAH HAH!"

Jesus Christ... This was unbearable. I looked over at Shawn to see his reaction. But he wasn't even watching the video. He was still watching me.

"Do you find this disturbing?" I asked. "Or do you think she deserves to be tortured for making jokes on Twitter?"

Shawn didn't react. He just kept watching me.

"For fuck's sake." I muttered, turning back to the video.

"I HAVE A FUNNY JOKE FOR YOU, MAGGIE!" The Chicken was shouting again. "DO YOU WANT TO HEAR IT?"

She let out a muffled sound, eyes watering.

"KNOCK KNOCK? WHO'S THERE!"

Then, without warning, The Chicken pulled out a large pair of scissors and lunged at her face.

What happened next, I couldn't quite tell. The camera was too shaky.

I don't wanna be a chicken... I don't wanna be a duck... So I shake my butt!

Maggie was screaming, and her face was covered in blood. To her side of her head, there was a chunk of flesh on the ground.

Was it her nose? Her mouth? Her tongue?

I never got a chance to find out.

As Maggie continued crying out in pain, The Chicken took back the camera's focus.

"Let's see... Debeaking has been a SUCCESS!" The Chicken held up the checklist again and crossed off the first line. "YES, VERY FUNNY JOKE INDEED!"

My heart sank as I read the remaining items:

1. Debeaking
2. Forced lactation
3. Slaughterhouse

PART TWO

I don't really want to talk about what happened next.

Yes, The Chicken crossed Item #2 off the checklist. I'm not comfortable describing any of it, but let's just say that forced lactation was... exactly what you'd imagine.

At this point, the stream had spread far beyond the island, with millions of viewers tuning in live. Festival participants seemed remarkably unfazed by the whole thing. I mean, sure, they were sharing thoughts and prayers with tear-filled emojis, but most people were out taking selfies by the beach.

Numerous sites had already removed the stream, but it just kept popping up like some sort of sick version of whack-a-mole.

With only "Slaughterhouse" remaining on the checklist, the stream had flipped to a black screen with an ominous countdown:

"Intermission: We'll be back in 3 hours 18 minutes 45 seconds"

That was how much time I had to get something — anything — out of Shawn.

"Okay, you need to say something," I spoke firmly to Shawn. "Did you not see what just happened to that poor girl?"

Shawn looked at me, expressionless, completely unaffected by what we'd just witnessed.

"They say you're not on the flight manifest," I said. "So how did you get here?"

Again, just a meaningless gaze.

How the hell had this person become famous?

I took out my phone and Googled 'silent person watching

animal abuse' and found Shawn's profile within seconds.

@HeartOfTheWorld103 - We all share one heart - Pronouns: he/him/his

I sorted by his top YouTube videos and clicked the most popular one.

Shawn Watches Culling: 8.4 million views.

The video was split in two. On the left half, there was a conveyer belt of baby chicks. On the right, it was just Shawn's face.

I watched uncomfortably as hundreds of chicks fell between the wheels of a macerator machine, killing them instantly.

I was surprised to see tears falling down Shawn's face. There was a deep sadness in his eyes — almost like he was experiencing their suffering as his own. Each one of his blinks was slow and drawn out.

Scrolling through the comments, I found a wide variety of feedback:

Shawn's heart breaks for the world <3
Chick-fil-A will cheer u up, stupid faggot.
God speaks through his eyes.
Who the fuck is Shawn? Like seriously where did he come from lmao
Shawn is mother nature's human form

And then some comments that I didn't understand.

No one:
Absolutely no one:
Shawn:

Looking back at the Shawn in front of me, there was a stark difference from the emotional man on the video. It wasn't like he was enjoying Maggie's torture, but I agreed with Zach that it was unsettling how he didn't seem to care at all.

Realizing that I wasn't going to get anywhere with him, I suddenly had an idea.

"I'll be right back."

I walked over to the door and peeked my head into the hallway.

"Noah, can you come in here for a minute?"

Noah perked up from the couch. "Me?"

"Yes, please."

It was a long shot, but Noah had a way of connecting with people who refused to communicate… normally. Something about the way his mind worked just seemed to automatically know what people needed.

"What's going on, Doc?" Noah met me at the door.

"The patient's name is Shawn," I said, ushering him inside. "He's doing a silent protest—"

"Yes, Zach showed me his profile!" Noah whispered back. "I watched all of his videos, just in case you needed anything."

"Oh — great," I said. "Yeah, I just figured you're good with silent people. Remember James?"

Noah's eyes lit up. "Of course!"

James was a lost young boy on the beach who refused to speak, but Noah somehow got him to open up within minutes.

Noah joined me across from Shawn and waved without speaking.

As expected, Shawn did not wave back, but he did turn his gaze from me to Noah. It was honestly a relief.

I watched curiously as Noah simply sat there and looked back at Shawn.

Noah gave him a gentle smile, but Shawn's expression did not change.

They continued like that for an uncomfortably long time, so I took out my phone in an effort to be less awkward. Making sure it was muted, I watched more videos of Shawn watching videos. They were all really difficult to stomach. Animals in cages where they couldn't even move, mothers forced to reproduce, crying out for their babies as throats were slit, and some factory workers laughing as wounded animals stumbled around.

Shawn's video reactions ranged from quiet crying to emotional sobbing to wincing in pain. But never anger. I *never*

26

saw anger in his eyes. Certainly not the anger of someone who could be involved with torturing a human.

"Okay, we're done!"

I looked up from the phone to see Noah looking brightly at me.

"You're… done?" I said. "You didn't get him to talk."

Noah frowned. "Well, no. He doesn't want to talk. But I think I know what we need to do."

"Of course you do." I said skeptically. "Well, let's hear it."

"Shawn would like us to try eating a vegan lunch today," he said. "Apparently little steps can make a big difference!"

"How can you — what?" I sputtered. "Do you think you have ESP or something?"

"No," said Noah. "I can just see it in his eyes."

"You didn't get that message from his creepy eye contact," I snapped. "You got brainwashed by the videos you've been watching all morning. This was a complete waste of time."

Noah sat up abruptly. "Please don't speak to me in a rude and dismissive way."

I nearly fell out of my chair. "W — What?"

"I'm sorry!" Noah's eyes went wide. "I've been trying to practice self-respect, and it seemed like you were being snippy with me, even though I was just trying to help. So I guess I was confused if I should stand up for myself. Or maybe you were joking? I'm not sure — sometimes it's hard to tell!"

From the corner of my eye, I noticed that Shawn was watching our exchange intently.

"Noah." I let out an exasperated sigh. "Level with me here for a second. A psychotic chicken just cut the lips off a young woman and harvested her breast milk. We have no leads, no suspects, no location, *nothing*. Then you come in here, make eye contact with my patient, and tell me to try a vegetarian lunch."

"Vegan," mumbled Noah.

I looked up. "What?"

"You said vegetarian," said Noah. "But it's supposed to be a vegan lunch."

I stared at him, at a loss for words.

"Oh my god." I buried my face in my hands, defeated. "Okay, Noah. Let's get some lunch."

While we waited anxiously for the next stream to start, we met Zach and Kierra at the buffet by the beach.

"So did you get anywhere with Shawn?" asked Zach as we moved through the line.

"No," I said, scooping some french fries onto my plate. "Like I said, therapy is hard when the patient doesn't speak."

"It's odd though, isn't it?" said Zach. "How stoic he is about the whole thing?"

"Sort of," I said. "But it's actually surprisingly common how many people struggle to watch animal abuse — and yet they don't even flinch seeing humans get tortured on TV."

"So you're not concerned about him?" asked Zach. "I really don't like that he somehow made it here without his name on the flight list."

"I mean, he was sitting in our room through the entire livestream," I said. "At worst, he's an accomplice, but he's definitely not that freaky chicken thing."

I took a bacon cheeseburger from the buffet and Noah cleared his throat behind me.

"What!" I said.

He crossed his arms.

Kierra pushed him aside and grabbed a burger as well. "I'm with the good doctor on this one. Life is too short for your sad plate of zucchini and strawberries."

I ignored her and found a seat outside near the water. If nothing else, this festival at least got credit for being hosted at a beautiful spot. A gentle breeze came off the clear turquoise water, bringing some calm to this otherwise chaotic day.

The others joined me shortly, but I was too distracted by my phone to hear their conversation. I took a bite of the burger and scrolled through Maggie Greenberg's Twitter feed, her last post was from yesterday: "Made it to the island, bitches."

Below it were seemingly endless comments about today's livestream. Some were supportive:

I'm so sorry you're going through this.
We love you Maggie. Hang in there.
They'll find the sicko doing this to you!
Guarantee it's some antifa leftie.

Others were just downright nasty:

Awww poor snowflake got a taste of her own poison.
Lmfao best stream of the year.
Anyone else getting a strange boner from this?

The more I read, the more I became convinced that Twitter was not a website I needed to join.

I scrolled back through her previous posts, looking for some sort of altercation or threat that might point us in the right direction. But she seemed to pick fights with *everyone*.

She apparently only posted on Monday afternoons, which her fans dubbed "Maggie Mondays"...

A week ago, black crime rates were proof that the entire race was dangerous.

The week before that, all trans people were mentally ill.

The week before that, being poor was a choice.

I try not to let politics cloud my judgment with a patient, but it was definitely safe to say she made a lot of enemies. When we're at war with the world, the world tends to fight back. But who fights back as a fucking chicken? And how was Shawn involved in all of this, if at all?

"What is going on in that big, beautiful mind...?"

I glanced up from my phone to see Kierra resting her head on one arm, gazing at me mysteriously.

I shot her a nasty look. "Would you shut up and let me think?"

"I'm just saying..." She sat up to take another bite of her burger. "You look a bit lost."

"I *am* lost." I dropped the phone on the table. "There are a million fucking people who hate this girl. Death threats on every single post. How are we supposed to narrow that down in three hours?"

"I have an idea," she said through a large mouthful of burger.

"Great."

"Why don't you stop playing detective..." She continued, chewing loudly. "And try doing your actual job."

"Kierra..." Zach warned.

"What!" said Kierra. "I'm just saying, you're sitting here reading through her social media like some sort of detective — or stalker ex. But isn't a therapist supposed to... I don't know... do something related to psychology?"

"There might be clues about her online!" I protested.

"There you go again!" She finished the burger, licking her fingers one by one. "Clues are for *detectives*. Last I heard, there are already detectives on the case — real detectives. Do you think they're dumb enough to miss her social media accounts?"

I stared at her.

"Right," she said. "So what exactly are you bringing to the table here?"

I realized that Zach and Noah were both looking at me, as if expecting me to answer the question.

"It just doesn't make any sense!" I said, exasperated.

"*What* doesn't make sense?" Kierra pressed.

"It doesn't add up," I said. "Activists are supposed to have a *message*. There's barely any message here. It's torture porn disguised as animal rights. These are crimes of *passion* — anger — there's so much anger. She's being abused, defiled, humiliated!"

"And...?"

"Well... What internet troll has that much hatred beyond a keyboard?" I said. "There are a million shitty people who say shitty things online — none of them are getting milked and de-beaked."

"So it seems personal to you?"

"It *is* personal!" I said. "It's extreme rage. More like a scorned ex or jilted lover than an activist. The whole vegan thing seems like a distraction."

"A misdirection, even…"

I jumped up, finally feeling energized. "I need to talk to Shawn. Can you guys ask the security team to check if any of Maggie's friends, former partners, or even family members are on the guest list? We need to stop looking at this as activism or terrorism — I think it might be a case of domestic violence."

Kierra stood up and bowed to an imaginary audience. "I'll be here all week, folks."

But before we could make any progress on this new theory, there was a retching sound from the adjacent table. I looked up to see two girls vomiting all over each other.

"What the…"

Surveying the lunch area, it was like some sort of mass plague had been unleashed.

Everyone was staring bug-eyed at their phones, crying, screaming, and throwing up. People were jumping up and running toward the ocean to vomit — turning the clear blue water into murky brown sludge.

"Oh my god."

I spun around to see Zach looking in horror at his phone. He slowly turned it to me, eyes haunted by what he'd seen.

The live stream had resumed, hours earlier than planned. But The Chicken wasn't in the same room anymore. And Maggie wasn't anywhere in sight.

"SLAUGHTERHOUSE SURPRISE!"

The Chicken stood in an industrial kitchen and zoomed in on a huge tub of ground beef. Then it began dumping in bags of something bloody and lumpy, and stirring it all together.

"HOPE YOU ENJOYED THE BURGERS!"

PART THREE

The following moments were a blur.

I joined dozens of other guests by the ocean, forcing myself to vomit into the water.

Every time I thought I was finished, my mind went back to that final video, and I threw up again.

Had I seriously just eaten a human being?

The nausea finally started to subside long enough for me to stand up and take a step back from the beach. Breathing heavily, I bent over and placed my hands on my knees.

So that was it. Maggie was dead.

I had completely failed.

"Christ almighty..." Zach stepped to my side, wiping bile from his own lips. "What the hell is going on, Elliot?"

"I don't know." I shook my head. "But we were too late. The countdown was just a distraction to get everyone to eat lunch. She was already dead."

"I can't believe I ate—" Zach retched and swallowed. "Christ. I should have followed their lead."

He pointed at Noah and Kierra, who were watching us from tables with concern. Well, Noah looked concerned. Kierra was chatting on her phone nonchalantly.

"Wait a minute..." I growled, making my way back to them.

"What?" said Zach, trailing after me.

"Why the fuck are you so calm?" I stormed up to Kierra, my face inches from hers. "I saw you eat that entire burger."

"Eh." She shrugged, lowering the phone. "It was cooked well-done. You know, normally I'd prefer medium rare, but I suppose in this particular instance, it turned out for the best—"

"YOU JUST ATE A FUCKING PERSON."

"As did you, Sergeant Shouty," said Kierra, raising her eyebrows. "The difference is that I'm not letting it ruin my day. Jeez... You'd think a therapist would know the power of positive thinking."

I stared at her and shook my head.

"She knows something," I turned to Zach. "She wouldn't be this calm unless she knew something about those burgers. Who was she talking to? I want to see her phone."

"Elliot, I know you're not a fan of hers—"

"This has nothing to do with that," I snapped. "That is not a normal fucking reaction to involuntary cannibalism. Zach, WHY is she here?"

Zach hesitated for a second, and then changed the subject. "Listen, I think we all just need to take a step back here..."

"Agreed," said Kierra. "We were making so much progress before we ate the patient. You were thinking domestic violence, right? So let's get started on that lead."

"She's DEAD, you insufferable bitch—"

"But..."

I was surprised to hear Noah speak up softly. We all turned to him.

"Well, she's right in a way, isn't she?" he said. "Shouldn't we still find Maggie's murderer? I mean, what if he hurts someone else? Isn't that the whole reason we're here?"

I bit my lip and realized he was probably right.

"Okay," I nodded reluctantly. "That's a good idea."

"Oh, sure," said Kierra. "When I suggest it, I'm an insufferable bitch. But when Captain Doofy says it, suddenly it's a good idea."

"*Good lord...*" Zach let out a loud sigh. "The two of you *have* to stop bickering."

I took a deep breath and decided to let it go, for now.

"Fine," I said stiffly. "So what's our plan here? I'm going to talk to Shawn, and you guys are going to check on close connections?"

"Actually..." said Kierra. "Before your little hissy fit, I was on the phone with the security team. Apparently they've already checked for friends, family, and exes."

"And?"

"Nothing," she said simply. "Nobody on the island has any links to her beyond casual social media followers."

"That doesn't make any sense!" I accidentally hit the table in frustration. "A random follower wouldn't do this. Something like this takes so much hatred — more hatred than any of us can fathom."

"The only person you've ever hated that much is yourself, am I right dick burner?" Kierra held up her hand. "Self-harm joke. Give me five."

Zach sighed again, but I suddenly felt tingles run up my spine.

"Come on, don't leave me hangin', Doc."

I surprised everyone by giving her an unenthusiastic high five and broke into a sprint.

Kierra had no idea — and I would never tell her this — but I was pretty sure she had just solved this patient file.

"Shawn, let's you and I have a little chat."

I sat down in front of him with a burger in my left hand.

Shawn eyed the burger curiously.

"You don't mind, do you?" I asked, raising the burger to my mouth. "I'm just really hungry."

I took a few bites, monitoring his reactions carefully.

"You look confused," I said through a full mouth. "I don't blame you. Why would I knowingly eat a burger made of human meat. I must be some kind of psycho, right?"

For once, Shawn's reactions were no longer stoic and expressionless.

"Unless… I was pretty damn confident there wasn't a person in here."

The quick flash of concern on Shawn's face was all I needed to continue.

"It's strange, we can't find a *single* thing about you online," I said. "No family, no history. Not even a last name. Just... Shawn."

Shawn did his best to appear calm, but he was becoming increasingly unsettled.

"It's like you appeared out of nowhere," I continued. "Just about nine months after Maggie Monday's got started."

I held up my phone to him and scrolled through Maggie's videos.

"A post every Monday. Starting in August. September. October..." I scrolled faster. "November. December. *January.*" I stopped scrolling at January. "Maggie Greenberg is from Vermont. But look at that — the trees in her window still have full green leaves. In January! I mean, I know global warming is bad and all, but that's a bit unusual, isn't it?"

Shawn swallowed.

"Unless, of course, all of the videos were pre-recorded over the summer," I said. "And then released on a schedule."

I put the phone down on the table.

"You can do a lot in nine months," I said. "You could learn to play piano... You could write a book... You could start to see noticeable results from hormone therapy."

Shawn's eyes went wide.

"You're not silent because of some activist strike," I said quietly. "You're silent because your voice hasn't dropped yet."

Shawn's expression was a mixture of fear and anger.

"Deadname," I said. "That's how some transgender individuals refer to their birth name, correct?"

Shawn pursed his lips.

"It's a powerful word," I said. "Represents the death of an old self. I've witnessed the process with several patients. But I've never seen someone actually *kill* their past self — let alone a public execution."

Shawn still wasn't speaking, but he seemed very upset now, and that was not my intention.

"No judgment here," I said, raising my hands. "God knows, I hated myself too — did some very unkind things to my body.

But we can find happiness from the pain. The first step is non-judgmental self-awareness—"

I paused, realizing that I had just quoted Noah.

"Try being compassionate with yourself, okay? We've all done shit in the past that we're not proud of. You're not Maggie Greenberg anymore. You don't have to hold yourself hostage forever. Self-forgiveness dissolves the shame."

Shawn's eyes began to water, but he blinked the tears back defiantly.

"So how did you do it?" I leaned forward. "You obviously recorded the Chicken videos before transitioning — some camera tricks for the torture, and stage makeup for blood. Then you used your birth name to fly here… Explains why there's no Shawn on the manifest. But how did you make it all look like a livestream? And who the hell was that Chicken person?"

Before Shawn could react, the security team barged in, trailed by Zach.

"You get anything out of him?" demanded Bruce Morgan, the head of security.

I looked at Shawn for another moment. His eyes were panicked, like a caged animal.

Then I turned back to Bruce.

"No," I said. "Nothing."

"Then pack your things!" Bruce barked at Shawn.

"What?" I interjected.

"Send the silent freak home!" shouted Bruce as he stormed out of the room. "And send the useless shrink home while we're at it. No fucking idea why he's here anyway."

"Sorry," whispered Zach. "He's just stressed from the burger incident. I'll talk to him."

Then he gave me a sympathetic look and clapped my shoulder. "Hey, no worries, Elliot. You'll crack the next case."

"Mhmm." I gave him a forced smile as he rushed to follow Bruce into the hallway.

Once again, it was just Shawn and I.

He looked up and gave me a cautious, curious glance.

"I'm not going to turn you in." I answered his silent question.

36

"I'm a therapist, not a detective. I have to file a report if I think you're a danger to yourself or others. But none of us ate Maggie Greenberg for lunch today, did we?"

Shawn shook his head.

"Right," I said. "So you're not a danger to anyone. In fact, revealing your past identity would probably put you in far greater danger. Maggie had some pretty nasty followers. We're better off with everyone thinking I'm an incompetent moron."

Shawn's expression relaxed a bit, but he still seemed anxious about something.

"Oh," I said, after thinking for a moment. "Don't worry about your voice. You're probably just a late bloomer. If you don't see any progress in the next few months, feel free to contact me. I'm confident we'll find something that works for you. The beard is coming in great, by the way."

Shawn's face lit up.

But before we could continue, Noah sprinted into the room.

"*Knock*, Noah…" I sighed.

"Sorry!" he said quickly, out of breath. "I heard Shawn was leaving, and I just wanted to — I just wanted to tell him something."

Shawn turned to him with a gentle expression.

Noah sat down next to me. "It's not anything big. I just wanted to tell you that you've convinced me to eat vegan for the rest of my life! I really love how much you care about animals. And I guess I was wondering if we could exchange phone numbers so we can stay friends?"

Shawn broke into a big smile and nodded.

Noah grinned and handed his phone to Shawn, who entered his contact information and gave the phone back.

"Thanks so much," said Noah, hopping up from the chair. "I'm sorry for interrupting. Hope you have a safe trip home!"

Shawn smiled again and waved goodbye.

"And I'll see *you* for our date tonight, Doc!"

Noah leaned in like he was going to give me a kiss on the cheek. I don't know why, but I instinctively ducked away. His ears turned bright red and he tried to pretend his kiss was an awkward whistle as he hurried out of the room.

Shit.

"Uh — so…" I turned back to Shawn, completely distracted. "Unless there's anything else, it sounds like they're going to send you home. And apparently me too. So… Best of luck with everything."

I extended my hand, forgetting that it was a futile gesture with Shawn.

But to my surprise, he accepted the handshake. And then to my total shock, he opened his mouth and started to speak.

"He is so in love with you," Shawn spoke softly, clasping his other hand around mine. "Please don't hurt him."

I stared back at him, unsure of how to respond to that. Why would I hurt Noah?

For once, I was the silent one.

All I could do was clear my throat uncomfortably as we stepped apart and walked out of the office.

But for the rest of the day, I couldn't get his words out of my head.

Why would I hurt Noah?

End of Patient File: @HeartOfTheWorld103

Our Second Date

Doc was running a few minutes late, so I checked myself in the mirror one last time — just in case. Not much had changed since thirty seconds ago. But just to be sure, I ran a hand through my hair and readjusted my shirt collar.

I took a deep breath, trying to relax the spastic guy in front of me.

"You got this, Noah!" I gave myself another pep talk. "You're a rockstar. It's gonna go great!"

I mean, sure, Doc avoided the kiss earlier. But maybe he just didn't feel comfortable doing that in front of a patient. Or maybe he wasn't even avoiding it! Maybe he ducked because of... something else. You just never know what's going on in someone's head.

There was a knock on the door, and my heart lit up with a combination of excitement and anxiety.

I ran over to let him, accidentally knocking over a lamp on the way.

"Hi-lo!" I said. "I mean hi — or hello. Sorry, I think I combined them."

Doc gave me a funny look. "Hi, Noah."

"Are you ready for our next date?" I asked, scrambling

to grab the necessary tools for our night.

"Are those... metal detectors?"

"Yeah!" I said, handing him one. "Don't worry, it'll all make sense soon."

He took his metal detector, still looking at me like I had two heads.

Then we made our way out of the building, heading toward the ocean. We didn't talk much, but that's okay! I read that some of the happiest couples spend *hours* in silence together. Can you imagine that?

We arrived to the beach and I took off my shoes, struggling with a sock as I stumbled into a bush.

Doc raised his eyebrows and took off his shoes as well.

"Wait a minute... Are we going to search for metal on the beach?"

"Perhaps!" I said, running onto the sand. "Finders keepers!"

He laughed and chased after me. "We're like old people."

We raced around the beach together, waving our metal detectors left and right in search of treasure.

Doc was the first to hear a beep.

"Got something!" he said.

I ran up next to him and watched eagerly as he dug through the sand.

"Wow..." he said, brushing off a small object. "This is actually a really nice pen. I could use it for my patient notes."

I gave him a smile. "Let's keep searching!"

He pocketed the pen and hurried after me, resuming our race.

A few moments later, his metal detector beeped again.

"It's some sort of charm!" he said excitedly, uncovering the next item. "A moon and a star. Awesome, I'm definitely putting this on my desk—"

Then he looked up at me curiously.

"Wait a minute..." he said. "Both of these are way too good to be random beach finds. Noah, did you bury these?"

I smiled again. "Maybe!"

He stared at me, mouth agape. "You didn't have to do all of this—"

"It was really fun!" I said, starting up my detector again. "But I think you're missing a few."

He broke into a huge smile and trailed after me. For the next twenty minutes, we uncovered all the treasure I had buried. An hourglass (to time his sessions — he said it's more subtle than clocks), a metal feather bookmark (he loves to read), a miniature hot air balloon (to remember our beach day), and a locket with a photo of us.

"Noah, this was such a cool idea," he said, gazing at the locket. "You're like some kind of expert at dates."

I felt my chest swell with happiness. "I'm so glad you liked it!"

We sat down in the sand, side by side, looking out over the ocean. The stars were so unbelievably bright and clear out here, without any light pollution from the island.

"The constellations here are different from home," said Doc enthusiastically.

He always got excited about stars.

For the rest of the night, he pointed out all of the different constellations, telling me stories and mythology about each one. I could have stayed like this forever.

It got quiet for a while, and then he turned to me slowly.

My heart felt like it was beating out of my chest. Was this the moment we would finally kiss again? I wasn't planning to initiate after what happened earlier, so the ball was in his court.

"Hey, what's the next key?" he asked.

"Oh!" I let out a nervous breath. "Fear friendship."

He raised his eyebrows. "What?"

"So a lot of people think fear is bad," I said, trying to forget about the kiss. "But I don't think fear is our enemy. Usually it just wants to protect us from getting hurt. Once we see that, we realize that fear is a friend, looking out for us. And that doesn't mean we have to listen to it all the time, but we also don't have to avoid it! Then everything relaxes a little bit."

Doc nodded and thought for a moment. "I love it."

I felt my cheeks go pink.

"Thanks, Doc."

In that moment, fear told me that he would reject any kind of advance, so I should just sit still and shut up. Fear told me that this could be our last date, and I might never get a chance to kiss him again. Fear told me that no one would ever love me the way I loved them, so I was better off alone.

I thanked the fear for trying to help me.

Then I reached out my quivering hand and put it on his.

Viral Germaphobe

Viral Germaphobe

PART ONE

With some patients, I don't come close to uncovering the issue. I don't ask the right questions. I don't see what's really going on beneath the surface.

I'm just along for the ride.

And that's precisely what happened with Linus Solomon.

"Please apply another squirt."

I squeezed a fourth round of Purell into my palms and rubbed my hands together until it dried.

"Good?" I asked.

Linus ignored me, continuing to walk through his checklist.

"Your vaccinations are all up to date?"

"Correct," I answered truthfully.

"And absolutely no diseases, viruses, or symptoms of a flu — or a cold?"

"Correct," I answered — completely untruthfully. I was HIV positive, but there was no reason he needed to know that. I didn't have any open wounds, and I certainly wasn't planning on sleeping with him. Medications made my viral load undetectable anyway, which meant transmission was nearly impossible.

Linus inspected me carefully and finally gave me a nod. He was about Noah's age, and at least twenty pounds underweight. His skin was unnaturally pale and his face was concealed by a surgical mask and goggles.

"Your temperature's a little high, but it doesn't look like a fever," he said, examining the thermometer that was just under my tongue. "You can join them in the kitchen. Put on the mask, and leave your phone in the safe."

I hesitated for a moment and put my phone in with the others. Then I fastened the surgical mask around my face.

I walked into the kitchen and found Kierra, Zach, and Noah — all masked up. It was honestly pretty creepy looking.

"You passed!" said Noah.

"Barely," I mumbled. "How did you guys get through so fast? That was worse than airport security."

Before we could continue talking, Linus walked over and reinspected our masks.

"How did you get all of this set up?" I asked, looking around in awe. It was like we were in some sort of underground fortress. Unlike all of the ocean-view bungalows, there wasn't a single window to be found in this place.

"Had it custom designed," he said proudly. "Told them I wouldn't come to the festival unless they met every specification. It's got medical supplies, food to last three months, twenty tanks of oxygen, and bulletproof walls."

"Wow, they did all that for you?" said Noah. "They must really like you!"

"They just like money," he said. "That was the deal. They build it, and I stream everything to my 12 million followers. They get the advertising revenue."

"That's actually why we're here…" I stepped in. "The festival organizers are a bit worried—"

"About my posts, I know," he said. "They keep sending me cease and desist letters."

"Would you mind sitting down with me for a few minutes?" I asked. "I'm sure you mean no harm. I just want to put their minds at ease."

"Sure," he said. "I've got nothing to hide."

He showed me into his office, and we left the others behind in the kitchen.

"Alright..." I said, taking a seat. "The thing is, after the whole chicken incident, they're taking threats pretty seriously right now."

"Good," he said. "They should be taking it seriously."

He handed the bottle of Purell to me, and I knew what to do.

"Linus," I said, taking another squirt. "Don't you think your posts are a bit... alarmist?"

For the past two days, Linus had been taking to Twitter and Facebook to warn about two guests at the festival. He claimed they had traveled to a Level 4 biolab immediately before arriving here at the island.

"They have location tracking enabled on their photos," he said. "Check the EXIF data yourself if you don't believe me. And they're researchers. What business do they have coming to a social media festival?"

"Couldn't they just have been... walking nearby?"

"You don't accidentally walk by a BSL-4 lab," he scoffed. "Those places are fenced up for miles."

"Okay." I decided to play along. "Let's say they *did* go to the lab, what do you think could happen?"

"Those labs handle the most dangerous and infectious viruses in the world," he said. "Ebola, coronavirus, Marburg, Lassa, Nipah, Crimean-Congo, HIV..."

I nodded with a pang of guilt.

"But if they're researchers, don't you think they would have taken precautions?" I asked. "You know, hazmat suits, masks, the whole nine yards. I'm sure they've got stricter policies than your fortress here."

"I would agree with you," he said. "If safety was their intention."

I raised my eyebrows. "You question their intentions?"

"Of course I do," he said. "These places spend decades and billions of dollars manipulating those viruses — repurposing them to become stronger and more infectious than nature ever intended. You think they'd invest all those resources without a plan to use them?"

"What would any government gain from unleashing a virus here?" I asked.

"Perfect place for a trial run on human subjects," he said simply. "It's an island. Anywhere else — even controlled environments — you run the risk of a pandemic. Here they can safely observe and learn."

I sat back in my seat and thought for a moment. Linus was obviously a germaphobe, but his conspiracy theories were bordering on delusional paranoia. It almost seemed like he *wanted* some sort of viral outbreak, so he could justify the drastic measures he'd taken to seclude himself from the world.

"Linus, I know how debilitating it can be to live a life dictated by fear," I began. "But there are so many ways we can—"

"I'm not afraid," said Linus. "I'm safe. The people on this island are the ones who should be afraid."

"See, that's exactly the kind of talk that's upsetting the security team," I said. "It almost sounds like you're threatening people, and we can't allow that."

Linus observed me through his goggles for a few seconds and then stood up.

"I think we're done here."

"What? No—"

"Thanks for stopping by," he said. "Good luck out there. I would get the hell off this island if I were you, before the quarantine starts and they block off the airport."

I trailed him back into the kitchen, surprised to see Noah, Zach, and Kierra glued to the television.

Linus slowed down and we turned to see a BREAKING NEWS banner flashing across the screen.

"Guests at the world's largest social media festival are facing yet another terrifying situation," the news anchor spoke quickly. "This video was uploaded just moments ago. Viewers are advised that the following content is graphic and disturbing."

The screen cut to a shaky cell phone video.

"What the hell is happening!" The girl recording the video let out a loud cough. "Oh my god!"

The video panned around and revealed a horrifying scene.

Dozens of panicked guests were running through hallways of the island's hotel building — where the cheapest rooms were. Most of the people seemed to be coughing, but it was hard to make out. Moments later, one person fell to the ground in a heap. The girl behind the video screamed and ran past the body.

Then the stream cut back to the anchor.

"We're getting reports from multiple influencers at the festival of a highly contagious illness sweeping the island," the reporter said. "Guests are advised to stay in their rooms and await further instruction."

Linus switched off the television and turned to face me.

"Believe me now?"

I shook my head and marched to the front door.

"We have to go help those people," I said. "This is probably some sort of food poisoning."

"Since when does food poisoning make people cough...?" said Kierra.

"I don't know," I snapped. "Just — Linus — open the door."

I turned around and realized that he wasn't following us. He was still in the kitchen.

"Linus," I said, marching back over to him. "Give us our phones and let us out of here."

But Linus paid us no attention, and instead was pressing buttons on a remote.

Suddenly a computerized woman's voice echoed through the fortress.

"Steel reinforcements. Enabled."

Linus slowly looked up at me, eyes peering through the goggles.

"No one goes in or out."

Then he shoved the bottle of Purell at me.

"Reapply."

PART TWO

"So what's his deal?" whispered Zach. "Is he some sort of hypochondriac?"

We were all huddled in the kitchen while Linus sprayed disinfectant around the fortress.

"I don't think so," I said. "Hypochondria tends to manifest in such a way that the patient believes they are *already* infected with a serious illness. Linus doesn't seem preoccupied with any symptoms in himself. But he's severely germaphobic, and definitely paranoid—"

"Paranoid?" Kierra laughed. "Is it really paranoia if he's correct?"

I glared at her. "He thinks this is a bioterrorist attack."

"Do we have evidence that it's *not?*" asked Zach. "It would explain all the death threats."

"This isn't bioterrorism!" I said. "We're on a confined island. Things like pneumonia and flu can spread quickly."

"But Linus was prepared for the whole thing," said Zach. "Isn't that a bit concerning?"

"Isn't what concerning?"

We all went silent as Linus joined us from behind.

"Nothing," I said quickly. "Just how quickly things are spreading."

"Well, that's what happens when a virus is engineered to be more contagious," said Linus. "I've finished sterilizing the premises. Can I get you anything to eat or drink?"

He was offering us refreshments like this was some sort of social gathering.

"Linus, we can't stay here," I said. "We need to go out there and help."

"That won't be possible," said Linus. "If the virus is airborne, your departure could contaminate the entire building. But don't worry, I have plenty of food and supplies to last us one full month."

"A *month*?"

"Well, it would have been longer, but now we're splitting the resources among five instead of one."

"We're not staying in this place for another hour — let alone a month."

"Dr. Harper, I understand your concerns, but as we learn more about this illness, I think you're going to find yourself quite grateful for your current accommodations."

"We can't learn a goddamn thing, because you've taken our phones."

I couldn't see his mouth behind that mask, but his eyes seemed to be smiling.

"Phones carry more germs than a toilet seat," he said. "And they won't work in here anyway. This entire complex operates as a Faraday cage. Our information will come from cable lines, which cannot be manipulated to induce radiation poisoning."

"For Christ's sake..." I breathed. "I swear to god, If you don't let us out right now—"

"Elliot." Zach reached out and placed his hand on my shoulder. "Let's just settle in for a bit, shall we? Something tells me that you and Linus will find plenty to talk about. You haven't had breakfast yet. Surely you must be hungry?"

I sighed and shook my head.

"Fine." I turned to Linus. "I'll take some eggs and orange juice."

"For breakfast, I have canned beans and powdered juice."

"Ugh." I stuck out my tongue. "Don't bother."

"Oh!" Noah raised his hand. "I'll have some!"

I rolled my eyes and stormed out of the kitchen, searching

for some sort of emergency exit.

We were not spending a month in this hellhole.

Eventually I gave up and accepted my fate, joining the others by the television — our only outside source of information about this mysterious illness.

There seemed to be a nightmare unfolding on the island.

The news continued to play videos from guests all across the island, panicked and confused. One particularly disturbing clip showed a group of men barricading a woman into her room as she coughed and begged for help. Within a few minutes, she had gone completely silent.

"Isn't it interesting how humans behave during events like this?"

We all turned to Linus, who was watching the screen with a strange look of fascination.

"Like clockwork, we turn on one another," he said. "Our primal tribal instincts become activated, and we make sacrifices to keep ourselves safe. We talk about freedom and compassion, but that all goes out the door in a mass extinction."

"Extinction?" Noah's eyes went wide as he inhaled his breakfast.

"Look at the facts in front of you," he said. "This illness is clearly airborne, and it seems to render the victim dead within a matter of minutes. The human race is not prepared for this. Only a select few will survive."

Noah dropped his fork, looking absolutely terrified.

"Anyone with half a brain would drop a bomb on this island," continued Linus. "Sure we'd all be obliterated, but at least—"

"Will you shut the fuck up?" I hissed. "You're scaring him."

Before we could get into another argument, the BREAKING NEWS banner broke out across the screen again.

"We're just getting word of a quarantine order for the entire island," said the anchor. "All planned flights and voyages have been cancelled until further notice. Once again, this illness appears to be highly contagious and dangerous. Guests are urged to stay in their rooms at all times. Should you encounter someone with symptoms, do NOT attempt to help them. Isolate yourself and call the security hotline listed at the bottom of this screen. You can find up to date details at the following website—"

But before we had a chance to see the URL, the screen flickered and displayed security footage — it appeared to be at our front door.

A young man was keeled over, coughing. A woman wiped her eyes and desperately hit the door buzzer.

"PLEASE HELP US!" Her voice blared on the intercom throughout the building. "IS ANYONE THERE?"

The five of us slowly turned to the door, and then to Linus.

He shook his head before anyone could even ask.

"Absolutely not."

"We need to help them," I said. "You have to let us out now."

"Didn't you hear the news?" said Linus. "They specifically said not to help anyone with symptoms."

"I'm with the creep on this one," said Kierra. "Why would we let the plague in here, where everything is safe and sound?"

"Because we're here to help people!" I said, turning to Zach. "Isn't that the entire reason we came to this island?"

He looked at me uncertainly. "Elliot, their instructions were pretty clear…"

"Are you fucking kidding me?" I snapped. "We have masks. And a gallon of hand sanitizer. We'll be fine."

Linus tilted his head curiously. "Do you have some sort of death wish, Dr. Harper?"

"Would you look yourself right now?" I stepped closer to him. "Huddled in this steel cage while innocent people out there are begging for help? The only infectious disease I see is fear.

What is the point of living if you're constantly afraid of death?"

"A healthy fear of death isn't the worst thing—"

"This isn't healthy!" I said. "You've been waiting for this moment your entire life. Now it's here, and you're going to camp out for a month eating canned beans. For fuck's sake. If you won't help them, at least let me out of here."

"I won't risk exposing—"

I grabbed a knife from the counter and slashed my palm open.

"I have HIV." I waved my bloody hand in Linus's face. "Let me out — or I'll make sure you get it too."

His eyes went wide and he bolted out of the room.

Zach and Noah shouted as I chased Linus around the premises, like a fucked up game of tag.

Finally, I caught him with my uninjured hand and yanked him into a chokehold with my bloody hand inches from his mouth.

"You're going to let me out of here," I said. "Right now."

He nodded and whimpered, reaching for his remote. He plugged in a few numbers and the computerized woman's voice echoed through the building:

"Front locks. Disabled."

I loosened my hold and he darted away, letting out a gasp of air as he drenched himself in Purell.

I turned to face the rest of the group.

"I'm going to help those people," I said. "Does anyone want to come?"

I stood there with my bloody hand spilling all over the floor.

Kierra leaned in closer to Zach and whispered, *"Why do we like him again?"*

"Hush, Kierra," he whispered back.

Then everyone went silent and stared back at me.

"Fine," I said, walking away. "Enjoy your life in the panic room."

"Wait!"

I turned around to see Noah trailing after me.

"I'll come!" He looked petrified, but determined. "I'll come with you."

"Noah, you don't have to…"

"No, I want to!" he said. "I want to help."

I nodded as I wrapped a bandage around my hand. "Okay. Let's do this. Make sure your mask is securely fastened, and remember not to touch your face."

"Got it." His voice cracked.

And so together, we walked to the main entrance, held our breath, and opened the door.

I could see Zach and Kierra watching cautiously from a distance. Linus was nowhere in sight.

"Oh, thank god!" The young woman ran up to us. "Everyone on the island is dying. We thought we got away, but then Barry started coughing."

"What's your name?" I asked as we hurried over to him.

"Jenna," she sniffled. "Oh my god, what is this? Some kind of virus?"

"Don't worry, Jenna, okay?" I said. "We're going to take care of him."

That seemed to encourage her a bit.

"Barry, can you hear me?" I asked.

He nodded and tried to answer, which resulted in another coughing fit.

"Okay, just stay calm and don't speak," I said, handing him a bottle of water. "You need to drink this water."

As Barry downed the entire bottle, I turned back to Jenna.

"When did his symptoms start?" I asked.

"About ten minutes ago," she said. "Just a few seconds after one of the maids coughed near him."

"So it spreads extremely quickly," I said. "But the good news is, you haven't contracted the illness. And neither have we. Which means you may have some sort of immunity. And our masks seem to be effective against the virus."

I was actually starting to feel very optimistic about this whole thing.

Until Noah coughed.

PART THREE

"I don't feel right, Doc…" Noah started wavering back and forth.

"Here, sit down," I said, trying to sound calm. "You're going to be okay."

He began coughing uncontrollably, and my anxiety started to take over. I was the one who downplayed this whole thing and convinced him to come out here.

"Zach, find us help!" I shouted over to the front door.

"I'm trying!" he said, waving his phone at me. "I keep getting voicemail. They're probably overwhelmed with calls."

"Leave the fucking building!" I yelled. "Run back and find someone who can help us!"

Zach hesitated for a second and then nodded, grabbing Kierra. The two of them went sprinting back toward the center of the island. Then Linus hurried over to the door and slammed it shut.

Noah was still coughing.

I rushed to his side with a bottle of water, and that's when Barry fell to the ground.

"HELP!" Jenna screamed. "Oh my god, somebody help us!"

I hurried over to check his pulse.

"He's still breathing," I said. "It looks like he lost

consciousness."

"What's happening?" she sobbed. "Is he going to die?"

"No," I said, trying to convince the both of us. "No, he's going to be okay. We just need to stay calm."

Noah's coughing was getting worse, and his eyes were becoming glazed over.

"Noah, I need you to stay awake, okay?" I said quickly. "Have some more water."

I poured the bottle into his mouth, but most of it just spilled down his front side.

"Please, Noah..." I begged. "Stay awake."

I don't think I'd ever been this scared in my life. Where the hell was the security team? We desperately needed supplies and medicine, but the only building near us was...

I turned back to the fortress and saw Linus standing there, watching us from the closed door.

"Hey!" I marched over to the fortress and pressed the intercom button. "Hey, didn't you say you have medical supplies in there?"

Linus did not respond.

"Isn't this your fucking wet dream?" I shouted, banging on the door. "Saving the world from an apocalyptic plague?"

He picked up a microphone and spoke inaudibly. Then his voice projected outside.

"I take no pleasure in this."

"Then HELP us!" I pleaded into the intercom. "I need adrenaline. And saline solution."

He glanced at me for a moment and then disappeared into the fortress.

I turned back to the others to see Jenna descending into hysterics, slapping Barry in the face. "WAKE UP!"

"Hey!" I hurried over and pulled her away from him. Then I gently repositioned her hand on his pulse. "We're getting help now. Can you keep your fingers on his neck like this and make sure you feel a beat every few seconds?"

She nodded, mascara oozing down her cheeks.

I turned to check on Noah who was coughing again and

closing his eyes.

"Fuck," I muttered. I was running out of time — and hands. Both of their conditions were worsening, and Jenna was completely useless.

I looked back at the fortress and saw Linus standing there with a box.

I ran over to him and said, "Thank you!"

He spoke into his microphone again. "I need you to back away from the door. Then I'll leave the box outside."

I pressed the intercom button.

"Linus, I can't force you to do anything, but there are two very sick people and I could really use your help out here."

His eyes went wide, like I had just asked him to commit murder.

"Please," I said. "I'm begging—"

I turned back to see Noah fall to the ground.

Giving one last desperate look to Linus, I sprinted back to Noah and rested his head on my lap. I checked his pulse and breath. Both okay, just like Barry.

But then Jenna started screaming.

What now?

I turned around to see Barry convulsing. His body and limbs were thrashing uncontrollably, and his mouth was foaming.

He definitely needed my help more than Noah now, but the selfish part of me wanted to stay with Noah and figure out how to prevent the convulsions from happening to him.

"HELP US!" Jenna screamed.

My eyes darted back and forth between them and Noah.

How was I supposed to make this decision?

But then, to my complete and utter shock, Linus appeared at their side.

"Pull down his pants," said Linus. "If this is what I think it is, he needs epinephrine. Now."

Jenna nodded and yanked his pants down.

Linus prepared a syringe and then lifted it above his thigh. He was about to inject the dose when Barry suddenly started spitting.

Or... laughing?

"What the?"

"Oh my god!" Barry jumped up from the ground. "You should see your face!"

"W — What?" Jenna stammered.

"I got you so good!"

"BARRY!!!!" She yelled, tears falling down her cheeks. "WHAT THE FUCK!"

I stood up and stepped in between them. "What the hell is going on here?"

"YOU'RE SUCH A FUCKING ASSHOLE!"

Barry continued laughing and removed a tiny device from his front pocket.

"Smile for the camera!" he said. "I told you I'd get you back. That's why you don't mess with the Bear-Man."

"HEY!" I stepped in between them. "What is going on here?"

"We — We run a YouTube couple's prank channel," said Jenna. "We're always trying to out-do each other. Barry pissed his pants in the last one when I tricked him into thinking someone broke into our home. Now he's —"

"This was a PRANK?" I felt my blood pressure rising.

"Best one yet!" Barry laughed.

"But the whole island—"

"ACE Inhibitors and Ambien in the water, baby!" Barry was so happy with himself. "The inhibitors make people cough up a storm, and Ambien... Well, you know."

"You — You drugged the water supply?" I said. "You do realize that's a *felony*?"

"This ain't the USA, buddy!" he said, turning back to Jenna. "Slap on the wrist at best. Doesn't matter, anyway. We're famous now! Gonna make a million bucks from ads alone!"

Jenna instantly stopped crying. "A million dollars? You really think so?"

He nodded, laughing and whooping.

"Oh my god, babe!" She started to laugh too. "This was definitely the best prank yet!"

He held up the camera. "Subscribe to our YouTube channel!"

"PrankLove806, bitches!" she added, sticking up her middle finger.

I stared at them both for a second and then I couldn't help myself. I clenched my fist and punched Barry in the face.

"Hey!" Jenna hurried to his side. "You can't do that!"

I squeezed my fist harder and exhaled slowly — trying to restrain myself from hitting her next.

"Hey!" Jenna shouted again, looking up. "You just *assaulted* him on camera! Apologize right now, or I swear to god we'll sue—"

But before she could finish her sentence, she fell to the ground in a heap next to Barry.

I looked at my fist in surprise. I was almost positive I didn't do that.

I slowly turned to Linus and raised my eyebrows. "Did you just...?"

He gave me a shrug.

"Let's go find a bed for your friend."

After we told the security team everything, Zach and Kierra returned to bring Noah to the hospital for some monitoring with the others. He was going to be fine, but he got a pretty heavy dose of Ambien when he mixed tap water into his powdered juice. He was babbling on like a lunatic when they took him away.

"I'm sorry I was such an asshole."

I stood with Linus at the front door of the fortress, saying our goodbyes.

"That's okay," said Linus. "I have to say... I've had a lot of therapists over the years, but you're different from the rest."

A gave him an embarrassed smile. "More yelling?"

"More yelling... more threatening... more punching..."

"Again, I'm really sorry—"

"There's no need to apologize," he said. "To be fair, you got me to come out of my shell. None of the others managed to do that."

"I really appreciate you helping us," I said. "That was very brave."

"Apparently not, since it was all just a joke."

"You didn't know that at the time," I said. "You thought there was an infectious plague — your worst fear — and you still came out to help us. That's as brave as it gets."

He gave me a short nod.

"Well, I'm going to head over to the hospital and check on Noah," I said. "Listen, it was nice to meet you and hopefully I'll see you around the island."

Linus raised his eyebrows. "I'm sure you won't. My flight leaves in twenty minutes."

I frowned. "You're leaving?"

"Of course."

"But it was all a prank!" I said. "A couple of jerks playing tricks. You were never in any real danger."

"No danger?" said Linus. "The biolab researchers are still here on the island. Nobody is safe."

"They've been cleared by the security team."

"Dr. Harper, I admire your unwavering faith in the security here," he said. "Especially after a girl was tortured on live television, and hundreds of guests were drugged in plain sight."

"Those were flukes—"

"Look at the evidence in front of you," he said. "They're incompetent. There is no security here. Just security theater."

"Linus, we can't live our whole lives in fear—"

"In the event of another emergency, you can take shelter here," he said, scribbling on a post-it note. "The entrance code is 74291."

"I don't think that'll be necessary."

"Take the code, Dr. Harper." He shoved the post-it note at me. "Something tells me that your troubles on this island have only just begun."

And with that, he fastened his mask, put on a fresh pair of

latex gloves, and walked out of the fortress without a single piece of luggage.

I never saw Linus Solomon again.

"I can't do this anymore, Noah."

"What do you mean?" He sat up from the makeshift hospital bed, recovering from his Ambien overdose. "We're all fine, totally fine... Just a little loopy!"

"This island is killing me," I said, shaking my head. "The patients are insane. It's just one attention grab after another."

"That's why we're here, Doc!" he said, slurring his words. Then he whispered dramatically: "*To save the island.*"

He sounded drunk, which suddenly gave me a slightly unethical idea.

"Noah, I've been meaning to ask you something..."

He broke into a stupid grin. "My hand in marriage!"

"No," I said. "Kierra."

He groaned and sprawled back into bed.

"Why is she here?" I demanded.

He started rolling around and messing up the blankets like a child.

"I can't tell you!"

"Tell me, Noah!" I said forcefully. "Tell me why Kierra is here — or I'm leaving the island."

He bolted up from bed and looked at me like a sad puppy. "Don't go!"

I rolled my eyes.

"Come on, what are you hiding?" I pressed. "Why can't you tell me?"

He looked genuinely conflicted, like he had been wrestling with this long before tonight.

Then he gazed into my eyes, swaying from side to side.

"Do you trust me, Doc?"

I looked back at him and sighed. He already knew the answer to that question. Since the day we met, Noah had become the antidote to my fear — a relentless source of integrity when others inevitably faltered. And here I was, trying to manipulate him in his inebriated state.

I leaned forward, untangled his blanket, and gently tucked him into bed.

He pulled the blanket over his head and peeked out with a smile. "You make my heart feel squishy."

I shook my head and walked over to the door to turn off the lights.

"Go to sleep, dummy."

End of Patient File: @SmartPrepper99

 Our Third Date

I shot out of the hospital bed and looked at the clock. 11pm.

Oh no! We missed our date.

I ripped the blankets aside and jumped out of bed, surprised to find that my footing was still a bit wobbly. Maybe the drugs hadn't totally worn off. But that didn't matter. There was still time for our date!

I hurried out of the room, ducking like a secret agent in case there were any nurses.

I started humming the *Mission Impossible* song and held my hands like a gun in front of me.

"DUN DUN... DUN DUN—"

I tripped over a hospital cart and fell to the ground.

The last thing I remembered was giggling to myself as I faded out of consciousness.

"Knock knock!"

The next thing I knew, I was standing outside of Doc's room and tapping on his door. I wasn't sure how I got there — or why there was an unopened bottle of vodka in my hand.

"Noah?" Doc opened the door, rubbing his eyes. "What are you doing here?"

"Our date!"

He raised his eyebrows. "Is that vodka?"

"Ah hah!" I clapped my hands together, suddenly remembering why I had the alcohol. "Doc, I seem to be intoxicated. And therefore you should also be intoxicated. Otherwise this would be a very strange date."

"Yeah, we wouldn't want that..." he said. "Noah, it's almost midnight. You should be resting."

"No, I'm feeling fit as a fiddle!" I said, squeezing past him to get inside. "Where are your alcohol glasses?"

"As opposed to regular glasses...?" Doc followed me into the kitchen. "Noah, I rarely ever drink."

"Me neither!" I said. "But, when in Rome... Or when in... Where are we?"

I poured him a generous serving of vodka and dug through his mini-fridge to find some seltzer.

"I call this a vodka with soda," I said, handing it to him.

"Wow... You should patent that." He took the glass. "Noah, I'm not drinking. And you're not staying. I'm in my pajamas! Here, I'll walk you back to—"

"Oh my god!" I said, mouth wide open. "You ARE wearing pajamas! They're very cute."

"Noah, come on—" he said, trying to usher me out.

"No!" I sat down in the middle of his floor and crossed my arms. "It's date night."

"Oh my god..." He rubbed his eyes. "If I have one drink, do you promise you'll go to sleep after?"

I looked up at him with a big smile and stuck out my pinky.

"Pinky promise!"

Another hour passed by without registering in my brain.

Doc and I were both now sitting on the floor. The bottle of vodka was by his side — getting noticeably more empty. And I seemed to be wearing a pair of his pajamas.

"I thought I almost lost you today, Noah..." he said, bowing his head dramatically. "Thank god it wasn't a real plague."

I looked at him for a few seconds and then let out a small laugh.

He peered at me curiously. "What?"

"Nothing!" I said, stifling more laughter. "It's just... How do you *find* these people!?"

He leaned forward, splashing some of his drink on the floor. "W — What do you mean?"

"Like, a fake plague? A human hamburger? And, I mean — someone ate your ear in prison, right?"

He thought for a moment and frowned.

Then he burst out laughing too, spitting his drink everywhere.

"Oh my god!" he said. "Someone *actually* ate my ear!"

I started laughing again. I couldn't help it.

"You're the weirdest therapist ever!" I shoved him playfully.

"Wait a minute..." He looked up at the ceiling. "I'm the weirdest therapist ever!"

For the next minute, both of us were laughing so hard that we started to cry. I had never seen Doc like this in all our years working together.

"Okay... Okay..." said Doc, wiping his eyes. "What should we do now?"

"You should finish the vodka," I said mischievously. "So we can play spin the bottle."

We both went silent.

I realized that the Ambien seemed to have shut down whatever part of my brain was responsible for fear.

"Spin the bottle?" he repeated nervously. "There are only two of us."

"Exactly!" I gave him another gentle push, trying to be as clear as possible about my intentions.

He sighed and backed away. "Noah, we can't."

I stood up and pouted. "Why don't you want to kiss me?"

I was shocked to hear the words come out of my mouth. Fearless or not, I was pretty sure I would regret all of this tomorrow.

Doc's face went red.

"I do," he said quietly, glancing away from me. "You know I do. It's just... It wouldn't be right."

"What do you mean?" I asked.

"You're all... messed up," he said. "Adorable, but messed up. I just want to make sure you don't regret anything."

I broke into a smile and knelt back down next to him. "Aww...!"

Then I started speaking in a British accent for some reason.

"Might I interest you in a hug then?"

He smiled back and put his arm around me. "I'll definitely take you up on that."

Another hour disappeared from my memory.

Now we were at the kitchen table, and Doc was looking at me like he was expecting something.

"Noah?"

"Yes, sorry!" I said. "What's up?"

He gave me a funny look. "It's your turn."

I looked down and saw some playing cards in my hand. "Oh. Umm... Go fish!"

He snorted. "Alright... that's it. Time for bed."

"What!" I said. "I promise I don't have that card. Go fish!"

He crossed his arms. "We're playing Old Maid."

"Oh." I said. "I knew that! Here, take this card—"

"Come on." Doc dropped his cards on the table and stood up. "I'll take you to your room."

I decided to stop protesting, because I was actually feeling really tired, and the memory loss probably wasn't a very good sign either.

"Okay." I slumped my shoulders and stood up to follow him to the door. He still had a drunken stumble, which made me happy.

We walked past Zach and Kierra's rooms and came to a stop at mine.

"I had a lot of fun tonight," said Doc as we stood outside my door. "Although I'm sure I'll pay the price with a massive headache tomorrow."

"I had fun too!" I said. "Thanks for being... a cool

guy."

Doc laughed. "Same to you."

I unlocked the door and was about to hug him goodbye, when he spoke again.

"Hey, it's our third date," he said. "What's the third key?"

"Oh!" I felt my whole body light up. I couldn't believe he remembered. "It's uhh... It's exploring the past."

He raised his eyebrows. "In what way?"

"Well," I said. "I don't like to blame parents for stuff, but I think our childhood can help us understand a lot more about ourselves! For example, what were your parents like?"

He went quiet.

I tried to give him some time to think, but a response never came.

"Doc?"

"Sorry." He cleared his throat. "Anyway. Have a good night, Noah."

I reached out to hug him, but he was already gone.

I frowned, but didn't think much more of it as I stumbled into my room.

I finally fell into bed and a million thoughts swirled all around me. Overall, it was a good night. We laughed a lot. We played games. And I was pretty sure Doc said he wanted to kiss me! So that was a huge bonus.

But I noticed something else tonight.

I noticed that even in his drunken state, Doc always seemed to be in complete control of every single thing he said and did.

And I wasn't sure if that was a good thing.

Zach

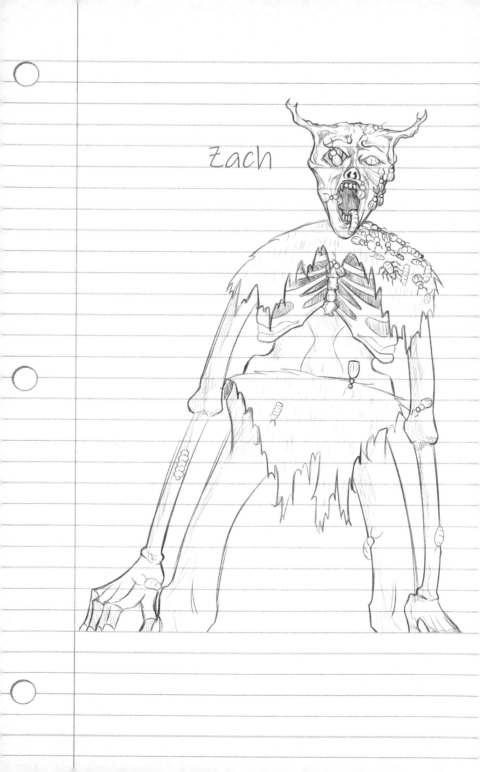

Zach

On the third day, there weren't any patients. No plagues, no crazy chickens, and no human burgers. Just people enjoying music (and presumably drugs) by the beach. The festival finally felt… like a festival.

So today, I'll share a story about my past.

There is no twist to this memory. No reveal, no red herring, no surprise.

It's just the story of two friends, who are somehow still friends. Hopefully it will help to explain why relationships don't quite come naturally to me.

"YOU CAN'T DO THIS TO US!"

I woke up to the sound of mom's muffled screams. This was not an unusual occurrence.

"YOU'RE ABANDONING US!"

I jumped out of bed and tiptoed to my parents' bedroom door, listening carefully.

"Not everything is abandonment!" I heard my dad's usual tone of exasperation. "I stayed as long as I could."

"You're abandoning your SON!" she screamed back. "WHEN HE NEEDS YOU MOST!"

"He doesn't need me!" he protested. "He doesn't even like me."

"He's your SON!"

"We have nothing in common!" My dad sighed loudly. "Ruth, he's — he's a weird kid. I stuck around through the gay thing, I stayed through the burning, I just… I can't connect with him."

I felt a strange knot form in my heart, but ignored it and leaned closer.

"You can't connect with your son so you abandon him?" My mom let out a chilling laugh. "WHAT A FUCKING DEADBEAT LOSER YOU ARE!"

"It's not just Elliot…" said my dad quietly.

"WHAT DOES THAT MEAN!"

There was a long pause. "You haven't done anything that the therapist recommended. You haven't gone to any of your DBT sessions. You've done nothing to improve your—"

"YOU'RE THE ONE WITH BORDERLINE PERSONALITY!" she shrieked. "YOU'RE THE DISORDERED ONE ABANDONING HIS TRAUMATIZED WIFE AND CHILD!"

"Jesus Christ…" Another loud sigh from my dad. "Listen, I'll send money. Whatever you guys need."

"FUCK YOUR MONEY!" she screamed. "FUCK YOU AND FUCK YOUR FUCKING MONEY!"

Something crashed to the ground.

"Ruth, stop," he hissed. "You're going to wake Elliot."

"Oh, NOW you're concerned about him!" she continued yelling. "What happened to ABANDONING US?"

"I'm not — I don't —" He always sounded so tired. "Ruth, this isn't what I signed up for. You're not the same woman I married."

"THAT'S BECAUSE YOU ABUSED ME!"

"I never laid a hand on you," he said firmly. "I supported you through everything. Do you have any idea how hard it is to watch your wife self-harm, and then see your kid start doing the same—"

"We're SO SORRY for INCONVENIENCING you with our pain!"

Another long pause. "I'm sorry, Ruth."

I heard footsteps approaching the door so I bolted back to my room.

"YOU'RE NOT GOING TO FIGHT FOR HIM?" My

mom's shouts continued. "YOU'RE NOT EVEN GOING TO SAY GOODBYE?"

There were more muffled sounds as they went downstairs. Eventually a door slammed shut, and there was a loud wail from the kitchen.

The stairs started to creak again so I closed my eyes, pretending to sleep.

"HE LEFT US!" My door swung open. "FUCK!"

My mom collapsed on the bed next to me.

I sat up. "Are — are you okay?"

"It was fine when it was just me and him," she sobbed. "But apparently when you started acting out, it was too much for him."

"I'm sorry," I stammered. "I — I didn't mean to."

The knot in my heart tightened as I realized that my out-of-control emotions were responsible for all of this.

"It's okay, love... I forgive you..." She sniffled and wrapped her arms around me. "We'll take care of each other now."

"Elliot, you okay? You look awful."

Zach and I were having our usual lunch together on the town docks, skipping stones into the lake.

"Just slept weird," I said. "But good to know I look like shit."

Zach laughed. "Sorry. Just wanted to make sure everything was okay."

"I'm fine," I snapped, chucking a rock into the lake with zero skips.

"Alright..." Zach raised his eyebrows. "So what's new with you? Ready for midterms?"

"I think so," I said. "Math is gonna be a bitch, but the rest should be okay. What about you?"

"I'm more worried about physics." He threw a stone perfectly and we watched it bounce across the calm spring water. "Sweet. Seven's the new record."

"That wasn't seven," I said. "Five at best."

Zach rolled his eyes. "You're such a sore loser."

I gave him a playful shove and reached down for my sandwich. He opened up his bag as well and we sat there for a while, just enjoying the peace and quiet.

This was the only part of high school that I actually liked — when the weather finally got nice enough for Zach and I to sneak away and hang out by the lake.

"Hey, did you hear Brandon came out?"

I put down my sandwich and glared at him. "I'm not doing this."

"What!" said Zach innocently. "I just wasn't sure if you heard the news."

I gave him an incoherent grunt and returned to my lunch.

"He's pretty cute though, right?"

I let out a loud sigh. "Zach, I don't need you to play matchmaker."

"Not a match!" he said quickly. "Just... You know — an attractive friend."

I threw another stone into the lake. Another failure.

"Isn't that the guy who's always running around in girl's clothes and makeup?" I said. "He's probably got Histrionic Personality Disorder or something."

Zach looked irritated, which secretly made me happy.

"Why do you always do that?" he asked.

"Do what?"

"Every time I try to introduce you to someone, you diagnose them with a mental disorder."

"I do not—"

"Yes you do!" said Zach. "You called Pete bipolar. You said Walter was schizophrenic. And I can't even remember the words you used for Carl."

"Co-morbid social anxiety with major depression."

Zach threw his arms in the air. "Exactly!"

"They're all true," I grumbled.

"Elliot, how are you ever going to enjoy people if you just keep searching for their problems?"

"I do enjoy people!" I protested. "I love people."

Zach reached for another stone and gave me a mischievous grin.

"Then you're going to love this."

I raised my eyebrows. "Love what?"

"I signed us up for drama club." He tossed the stone. "Eight!"

"You — what?"

"Hey, you love people so much," he said. "What better way to meet more people?"

"Why drama club?" I said. "Are you hoping I'll meet all my fellow gays there?"

"No — I — " Zach looked down awkwardly. "I just think that club has a lot of cool people."

"I'm not going," I said. "I can't stand drama kids. Always belting annoying songs and trying to get attention. Seems like they all have—"

"I swear to god, if you diagnose an entire school club right now..."

I stopped talking and skipped a rock. Two bounces.

"They meet during lunch anyway," I mumbled. "Why would we trade this for that?"

"Because it could be fun!" he said enthusiastically. "And hey, you might find someone you really like!"

I spun around, suddenly overwhelmed by that mysterious pressure in my chest.

"Why do you keep trying to hand me off?"

Zach frowned. "What?"

"You obviously want me to find a friend or boyfriend or whatever so I'll leave you alone," I said, unable to stop the poison spewing from my mouth. "If I'm such a burden, feel free to leave."

Zach gave me a strange look. "Elliot... What are you talking about?"

"I don't blame you," I said. "If I were you, I wouldn't want to spend my time with a depressing loser who had a crush on me."

Zach stared at me, shook his head, and stood up.

"I don't know what's going on with you today, but I'll be at drama club tomorrow," he said. "Hope to see you there."

"Have fun, asshole."

I thought I said it quietly under my breath, but Zach stormed back to the edge of the dock and kicked the rest of my lunch into the water.

I carried two bowls of pasta and veggies in from the kitchen. My mom wasn't well enough to cook, so I had taken up some of the household responsibilities while she recovered.

"Thank you so much, Elliot." She sniffled and took the bowl. "You're an angel."

She took a few bites and then looked up at me. Within seconds, her eyes started to water.

"You know what really gets me?" She broke into uncontrollable sobs, and I ignored a growing feeling of dread inside of me. "All these years — he was just *tolerating* you. He kept saying that he 'stayed as long as he could' and 'stuck around' through your phases, like it was some sort of *chore!*"

I felt that familiar discomfort in my chest, and I didn't know how to respond. I was disgusted with myself for hogging up so much attention with my ridiculous childhood drama.

"Maybe he'll come back?" I suggested hopefully. "Sometimes people just need a break, right?"

"No." She shook her head miserably. "No, this time it's permanent."

"I could try to talk to him," I said. "Maybe if I —"

"No!" She bolted upright. "He's dead to us, do you understand? I don't ever want you contacting him again."

"Okay." I nodded.

"Promise me, Elliot!" She shook my shoulders.

"I promise."

"Good." She let out a loud sigh and relaxed back onto the couch. "It's just us now. We have to look out for each other."

We spent the rest of the evening watching TV. My mom

didn't touch her dinner, so I cleared the dishes and put her pasta into Tupperware for tomorrow.

When I returned from the kitchen, she was sound asleep — sprawled out on the couch with the remote slipping from her hand.

I hurried over to catch the remote before it fell on the ground. Then I dug out a few blankets from the cabinet and gently draped them on top of her.

I flipped off the TV, turned down the lights, and made my way upstairs.

Laying in bed, I couldn't seem to shut down my mind. I know she said not to contact my dad, but what if I could convince him to come back? What if I could undo this whole mess?

Heart racing, I opened my cell phone and composed a new message.

I wrote out a few sentences, and then rewrote it. Then rewrote it again. Then rewrote it a dozen more times.

I finally settled on this:

Hey dad, it's Elliot. Just wanted to say I hope you're okay. And sorry for everything. Love you!

Cool. Calm. Casual.

I hit send and felt a lump in my throat.

I closed my phone and then instantly reopened it to see if there was a response.

Nothing.

I realized that he might be at dinner, so I decided that I would need to find something to occupy my mind while I waited. I remembered that Dr. Cole used to recommend journaling through difficult emotions. I didn't have a journal, but I had plenty of notebooks for school.

I dug through my bag and grabbed my math notebook, which only had notes from the first four days of school.

Before I started journaling, I checked my phone again — just in case.

Nothing.

"Okay," I muttered out loud. "Focus, Elliot."

I stared at the blank notebook and brought my pen close to the page.

Dr. Cole said to write about feelings and emotions, but those were exactly what caused this whole situation. So what was I supposed to put down?

I continued looking at the empty page for what felt like an eternity, until finally giving up and tossing the notebook on the ground.

I checked my phone again.

Nothing.

Maybe he was working late?

But with every minute that passed without a reply, an agonizing sensation coursed through my entire body. The only remedy seemed to be distractions. So I set a timer on my phone and vowed not to check until it expired.

I grabbed a book from my bedside table and tried to read. I made it a few pages, only to realize my eyes had been scanning the words without actually reading them. I restarted a few times, but the same thing kept happening after a few paragraphs.

At this point, I was so desperate for distractions that I decided to get some homework done for the week. I worked on a few midterm projects absentmindedly, and that finally did the trick. The minutes started to pass, and before long, I lost track of time. Until —

Buzz. Buzz.

It felt like someone had hit me with a dose of adrenaline.

I jolted up from my notes and grabbed my phone so quickly that I almost knocked it off the bedside table.

But it wasn't a text. It was just the timer.

I let out an accidental whimper and fell back into bed. I knew this wasn't sustainable. It was already midnight and I desperately needed to get some sleep.

I shut off the lights and turned up the phone's volume — just in case.

I closed my eyes, but I don't know if I ever really fell asleep.

At some point, my subconscious took over and introduced me to a screaming demon that lived under my skin. Spitting bile and insects, it hated everyone and everything, especially the people I thought I loved. They were all disgusting, pathetic failures. Frauds and fakes.

Then, together, the demon and I produced a blowtorch and aimed it at my genitals.

"BURN, ELLIOT."

I bolted out of bed, breathing heavily.

What the hell was that?

I took a few deep breaths, just like Dr. Cole taught me.

"It's okay..." I panted. "You're okay... Just—"

But before I could finish, the demon suddenly tore itself out of my heart, splitting my ribcage all over the bed. Then it brought itself face to face with me, and opened its mouth to reveal a black hole of disease and suffering.

The voice was endless and guttural. It did not come from this world.

"I AM YOU."

Then it ripped out my eyeballs and dove straight into the bloody sockets, screaming with rage and delight as it consumed me.

Once again, I jumped up from bed. This time I was soaked in sweat — at least, I hoped it was sweat.

Fuck.

I wiped away tears from my cheeks and took a few shallow breaths.

Was I finally awake? Or was that thing going to come back again?

And then out of the corner of my eye, I saw it.

The phone.

I reached for it and closed my eyes, hoping — maybe even praying — for a reply.

I opened it.

My eyes stung as I looked at the blank screen, but I refused to surrender to the sadness.

"*Maybe tomorrow,*" I told myself.

As I settled back into the drenched sheets, I closed my eyes and tried to stay optimistic — just like Dr. Cole taught me.

Maybe he left his phone in the office. Or maybe he fell asleep early. Or maybe the message didn't go through.

But deep within my heart, there was a festering black rot that told me the truth.

The next day, I arrived at the dock with my bagged lunch and notebook, ready to finally get some journaling done.

Zach was nowhere in sight, as expected.

"See?" I muttered to myself, taking a seat. "Everyone leaves if you give them a chance."

Once again, I was unable to think of anything to write down in my notebook. So I bit into my sandwich and grabbed a couple of leftover stones from yesterday.

The first two sunk immediately.

The third one made it a hop before disappearing beneath the surface.

How was I so fucking bad at this?

I grabbed another stone and raised my arm in frustration. But before I could throw it, a different stone went flying past me and bounced all the way to the middle of the lake.

"Seven."

I spun around, surprised to see Zach standing behind me.

"Scooch over."

I reluctantly moved to the side and made room for him. The fact that he came here and disproved my conspiracies made me feel embarrassed about my behavior yesterday. Goddamm Zach and his desire to be a good person.

"Why aren't you at drama club?" I asked quietly.

"Well, I was," he said. "But I couldn't find my friend there."

"Who's your friend?"

Zach stared at me incredulously. "You, Elliot."

"I know," I mumbled. "I'm just being a jerk."

"You really are..." said Zach, moving a bit closer to me. "Elliot, what's going on with you lately? Are you sure everything's okay? You know you can tell me anything, right?"

My eyes suddenly started to burn.

In that moment, I wanted to burst into tears and tell Zach everything. I wanted to hug him and tell him that my dad left, and that it was all my fault. I wanted to tell him that I had ruined our family. I wanted to tell him about the agonizing pain that tore through my nightmares last night. I wanted to tell him that he was the only stable thing left in my life, and that I loved him more than words could describe.

My brain quickly played that scenario out and calculated all the risks of opening up like that.

No, that wasn't a good idea. I refused to surrender to the sadness.

So I swallowed and felt the knot in my heart solidify.

"It's all good," I said. "I've just been sleeping like garbage lately."

Zach eyed me suspiciously but did not push the subject further.

"It was a cool group of people," he said. "They're working on some sort of improv show."

"Sounds terrible," I mumbled, playing with my food.

Zach bit down on his lip, clearly holding back.

"What?" I egged him on, feeling the pressure build back up inside of me. "Is there something you want to say?"

"I don't get you!" Zach blurted out.

"You don't *get* me?"

"It's like — It's like you've decided there's something wrong with you and therefore don't believe *anyone* could like you."

"That's not true!" I sat up defensively.

"Yes it is!" he said. "I'm trying to prove that I love being your friend, but it makes no difference. Nothing I do convinces you of it. You keep diagnosing everyone with problems, but maybe it's time to focus on yourself."

"Why did you even come back here?" I demanded. "To make me feel like shit?"

"You're already doing a good job of that yourself, aren't you?" he said. "I came back because I was worried about you."

"Well I don't need your charity," I snapped. "Go hang out

with your new friends. I'm sorry I inconvenienced you."

Zach stood up and shook his head. "You're impossible."

"Don't worry," I said, dripping with insincerity. "You can still feel good about yourself for coming back here to check on the loser. You're *such* a good person, Zach."

As Zach stormed away, the discomfort in my chest raged, but I dismissed it. He was so flakey and unreliable. Why did he need to be friends with everybody? Why did he constantly have to be taking part in some activity? Why couldn't he just sit still and enjoy what he had?

Honestly, it seemed like he might have ADHD or something. At this point, it was getting hard to keep track of everyone's problems.

I raised my eyebrows, suddenly consumed by an exciting new idea.

I tore open my notebook, clicked the pen, and scribbled down:

Patient File #1: Zach

Our Fourth Date

I took a deep breath and closed my eyes as I knocked on Doc's door.

I hadn't seen him since last night, and I was so embarrassed about my behavior. I couldn't believe I threw a tantrum and demanded a kiss. Who does that! Even though I knew our short relationship had probably come to an end, I still wanted to come here and apologize in person.

Doc opened the door without speaking and gave me an awkward smile.

Another few moments of uncomfortable silence followed, as neither of us seemed willing to start the conversation.

"I'm so sorry about last night!" I finally blurted out. "Oh my gosh, you must think I'm such a weirdo. I can't believe I said all of that stuff. I've seriously been cringing about it all day long—"

"Noah..."

"And jeez, I tried to make you play spin the bottle with two people. That's not even subtle! What in the world was I thinking—"

"Noah..."

"And then I forgot what card game we were playing, in the middle of the game! If you don't want to date me anymore, I totally understand—"

"Noah!" Doc raised his voice.

I looked up, eyes wide. I also realized that I was shaking.

"I had a lot of fun with you last night," he said gently. "And it's not your fault someone spiked your water with a mega-dose of Ambien. That would make anyone a little... goofy."

"Wait — you — you aren't dumping me?"

He gave me a funny look. "Why would I dump you? I've been waiting all day for our date."

My heart flooded with relief, and I think the color finally returned to my face.

"Oh my gosh!" I breathed. "Wow, okay! Great! I'm really excited for our date too. It's going to be so much fun! Especially now that I'm not intoxicated and stumbling all over the place like an idiot. Come on, follow me!"

I spun around and tripped over my shoelace, hitting the ground face-first.

———————————— // ————————————

"Noah, where in the world are you taking us?"

I gave Doc a mischievous grin as we slowed down at our destination in the middle of the jungle — at the edge of a cliff.

"Welcome, boys!" Xena, my new island friend, stepped out and greeted us. "Are you ready for the ride of a lifetime?"

Doc frowned. "The ride of a... what?"

"The world's wildest zipline!" said Xena enthusiastically. "A complete tour of the island from south to north. You'll see it all! Jungles, waterfalls, villas, and the open ocean."

Doc's face went white. "What!"

"Normally we don't run rides at night, but Noah here *insisted* that you were special."

Doc turned to me and whispered, "Noah, I'm terrified of heights!"

"I know, me too!" I said. "I figured this could be a great way for us to conquer our fears together."

He swallowed as Xena led us to the zipline and buckled us in tight next to each other.

"Now, your feet are going to dangle freely, but don't worry about a thing. You're strapped in and protected by three separate failsafes. So sit back, relax, and enjoy the show!"

With that, she stepped away from us and went into the booth. For a few seconds, nothing happened. And then there was a tiny sound:

Click.

"AGHHHHHHH FUCK SHIT JESUS FUCK CHRIST FUCK!!!!!!!"

Doc screamed at the top of his lungs as we flew across the night sky — legs hanging down below us.

"Oh my gosh!" I shouted back, laughing in terror. "This is crazy!"

Doc continued screaming for a little while, but eventually transitioned into panicked breathing.

"Is that our villa?" I yelled, pointing to the coastline.

"I don't know!" Doc's eyes were closed.

As we continued soaring through the open air, I pointed out more landmarks and Doc's eyes eventually quivered open.

He took one look around and grabbed my hand tight, which could not have made me happier.

I squeezed his hand back and leaned a little closer. This was probably not the right time to attempt a kiss — since Doc seemed sort of traumatized — but I could have held his hand like this forever.

"Is that Linus's fortress?" Doc called out, pointing to our side. "Why are the lights on?"

I followed his gaze but we were moving so quickly that I didn't really get a chance to see.

Next, we passed over waterfalls, followed by dance parties and romantic dinners at our feet.

And finally, with an abrupt *CRACK*, our adventure came to an end.

We swung back and forth a few times, before settling onto the platform.

"How was your ride?"

A young man came over and unclipped us from our harnesses.

"Amazing!" I said as we stepped out. "Thank you so much for letting us do this at night!"

I reached into my pocket and handed him a tip.

"Appreciate it," he said with a wink. "You gentlemen have a good night now."

Doc and I made our way to the path, legs a bit wobbly from the trip.

"So!" I said. "Did you have fun?"

Doc slowed down and turned to face me. Then, to my complete surprise, he looked up into the sky and started hollering.

"WOOOO! I FEEL ALIVE!"

I raised my eyebrows and laughed. "You're an

adrenaline junkie!"

"Fear is my friend!" he said, grabbing onto my shoulders. "Noah, I think I'm ready for the next key."

"Wow, okay!" I said. "You'll like this one — you already do it all the time. It's fighting against injustice. When we work on improving ourselves, I just think it's really important that we stand up for people who can't stand up for themselves."

He looked back to the sky and spun around in a circle. "I... LOVE IT!"

I laughed again. "Doc, I've never seen you like this!"

He leapt forward and pulled me into a tight embrace, looking directly into my eyes.

"I want to kiss you, Noah."

My heart — and other areas — surged with excitement.

"Oh — Okay!" I stammered.

I closed my eyes as he leaned in. I couldn't believe it was finally happening. And I *really* couldn't believe Doc was the one initiating it. This was like a dream come true.

"Guys!"

My eyes shot open and Doc pulled away from me.

It was Zach.

"Sorry to interrupt," he said, out of breath. "But we need your help."

"What — uhh..." Doc brushed off his shirt, looking very flustered. "What's going on?"

Zach bowed his head.

"There's been a rape on the island."

Cancel Culture

Cancel Culture

PART ONE

"Have you ever been accused of rape, Doctor?"

Rocky was an unusually attractive middle-aged man, sporting a tight t-shirt that made it clear he went to the gym. A lot.

"No," I said, thinking for a moment. "That's actually one of the few things I haven't been accused of."

"All it takes is one lie," he said. "One lie to ruin your entire life. Doesn't matter if it's true or not. It sticks forever."

"Nobody's accusing you of anything here, Rocky. We just want to talk with you."

He scoffed. "Right. Someone's been raped, and you just want to *talk* with me."

I leaned back in my chair and nodded. He didn't trust me — or anyone — and that made sense. I had briefly read through his story before our session, but it would still help to hear his perspective.

"Rocky, can you tell me exactly what happened two years ago?"

He clenched his fists.

"I'm a firefighter. I got called to a fire in the middle of the night," he said. "I show up and there's no fire. Just a cat and an old lady, passed out. I called the paramedics and they took her to the hospital. The end."

"But what about her accusations?"

"Fuck them!" he said. "Lies. Fucking lies. They don't deserve our time."

"It would really just help me understand where you're coming from."

"Fine," he said. "Later that day, the police surround my house. She claimed she woke up with a firefighter on top of her — inside of her... mouth."

"What was going on through your mind then?" I asked.

"Panic," he said. "Shock. Disbelief. Confusion. I'd never hurt a woman, let alone an old lady."

"And what happened next?"

He looked down. "The fucking rumor mill. Someone leaked the story online. I logged in to see my face trending with #GrandmaRapist. Next thing I know, I'm receiving thousands of messages telling me to kill myself — threatening to kill me."

"You had a big online presence?"

"Sort of." He shrugged. "Couple hundred thousand followers from firefighter calendars over the years."

"And then they all turned on you?"

"That's an understatement," he said. "Lost half of my followers in a day. The rest just stuck around to harass me. People started showing up outside of my building."

"What about the evidence?"

"What about it?" He laughed bitterly. "By the time the DNA results came out, it didn't matter. Everyone had already made up their minds."

"And that's when you started your non-profit?"

"Yes," he said. "Un-Canceled. It's for innocent people who have been persecuted by the social media lynch mob. We use all of our funds for marketing and publicity to help victims rebuild their reputation."

"How do you determine the innocent from the guilty?" I asked.

"Depends on the situation," he said. "In my case, the DNA tests proved it was her goddamn grandson. Sick fuck. That's why we're fighting for Rapid DNA testing kits everywhere, because every minute counts when you're combating misinformation."

"Well, clearly whatever you're doing is working," I said. "You're here, serving as a firefighter at the world's largest social media festival."

He snorted. "I'm here for one reason, and one reason alone."

"What's that?"

"Lawsuits," he said. "Another big part of Un-Canceled is holding social media platforms legally and financially responsible for enabling the spread of misinformation. And it's working. They're just trying to placate me with this firefighter gig."

I tilted my head and looked at him for a while.

His story added up. The evidence was on his side. But what were the odds? What were the odds of another elderly woman on this island being attacked — in the exact same way — with him here?

He smiled. "There it is."

"There what is?" I asked.

"The suspicion," he said. "Like I said, it never goes away. Doesn't matter how many times I prove my innocence. I'll always be a rapist to the world."

"I'm not—"

"That's okay, you don't have to explain yourself," he interrupted me. "But I will ask you to watch this."

He opened his phone and scrolled for a bit. Then he handed it to me.

I watched curiously as a LiveLeak video displayed a shaky video with a group of people standing outside an apartment building.

"COME OUTSIDE, RAPIST COWARD!" the cameraman shouted. The group started yelling in agreement and throwing stones at the window.

After a few minutes, Rocky came to the door. "I didn't do it!"

"RAPIST!" The cries became louder. "GRANDMA RAPIST!"

"I swear, I would never—"

Then a young woman from the group stepped forward with a metal bucket of liquid and hurled it at his lower torso. "NEVER AGAIN!"

He broke into agonizing screams and fell to the ground, writhing in pain.

The video ended with the group hooting and hollering while they kicked him.

I looked up from my phone and had to stop myself from gasping.

Rocky was standing in front of me — pants dropped.

Every inch of skin was mutilated and burnt, from his stomach to his inner thighs.

And there was a gaping hole where his penis should have been.

PART TWO

"Two burnt dicks on one island," said Kierra. "What are the odds?"

I ignored her and turned to Zach. "Did they find anything on the security cameras? Anyone who left or entered the building? "

"No." He shook his head. "Apparently the footage during that time got corrupted."

I did a double take. "Are you serious?"

Zach sighed. "Elliot, please don't get started with your conspiracies..."

"Are you kidding me?" I hissed. "You honestly believe that the security cameras just happened to crap out at the exact time this happened?"

"Elliot—"

"We need to get those tapes. If you guys distract the security team, I can check—"

"No," said Zach firmly. "No, I'm not comfortable with that."

"Fine," I said. "When we talk to the elderly rape victim, I'll tell her that we couldn't pursue every possible lead because it made you *uncomfortable*."

Zach stared at me. "You're such an asshole sometimes."

"Sometimes?" said Kierra.

"Now," I said, ignoring them. "All we need is a plan. There will probably be one or two guys at most in the surveillance room. We just need something to draw them out."

"I could tell them jokes?" offered Noah.

"No..." I said. "That's — weird."

Zach sighed. "I can make up a lead to distract them. I'll tell them we found something on the beach."

"Hmm... Better," I said. "But what if they already have people patrolling the beach?"

As I stood there trying to brainstorm, Kierra cleared her throat.

"What?" I snapped.

She let down her hair and tugged down her blouse, pushing her breasts together.

"Maybe I could be of assistance?"

———————————————— // ————————————————

"This is such a bad idea..." whispered Zach. "They're going to kick us off the island."

"Shhh," I hissed.

We stood outside the video room, and I motioned for Kierra to do her thing. It killed me to admit it, but her sex appeal was probably our best option here.

She gave us a wink and knocked on the door, while the rest of us peeked out from a broom closet across the way.

The door opened.

"Can I help you?" The guard spoke.

"Oh, sorry! I must have gotten the wrong room." Kierra's voice was as fake and innocent as ever. "Some guy at the beach said this was his room number. We were planning to meet up tonight and — oh, never mind..."

"No problem," said the guard, closing the door.

"Why are all men pigs?" said Kierra quickly, leaning closer to him. "They say they want one thing, and then they disappear."

"I don't — I don't know," he said. "Guys can be jerks."

She sighed dramatically. "For once, I wish I could just meet someone who doesn't want me for my body, you know? I mean, sure, I'm a wild ride in the bedroom—"

"*Real subtle...*" I grumbled.

"—But I'm so much *more* than that!" Kierra continued. "And yet... Here I am. Alone and lost on a foreign island. Anyway... I better get going. I can hardly make heads or tails of this place at night."

She waved and turned away, and my heart sank as the guard closed the door.

But then it swung open and he jogged after her. "Miss, you shouldn't walk home alone. Let me take you to your room."

"Oh, you're a saint..." she said, wrapping her arm around his.

As the two of them strolled away, I could have sworn she held up her middle finger behind her back.

"Okay," I said, pushing out of the closet. "We have to be fast. Noah, keep a close eye on the door."

We hurried into the security room, which consisted of nothing more than a chair and a dozen monitors.

"It's got to be that one," I said, pointing at the top right camera. "The victim had a beach villa."

Zach nodded and hit the rewind button.

It went back an hour, and then it turned to static.

"See?" said Zach. "I told you."

"Bullshit," I said. "Noah, grab the tape so we can figure out who tampered with it."

Noah didn't respond.

I turned to the door and saw Noah standing there, bright red.

"Sorry guys..."

He stepped aside to reveal Bruce — the head of security — with a gun to his back.

———————————————— // ————————————————

"Why is it always you four at the center of this goddamn clown show?"

Bruce Morgan looked like a combination of steroids and hypertension. I couldn't tell if he was overweight or muscular, and his face (along with his bald head) all seemed to be a permanent shade of purple.

It felt like we were at the principal's office. Noah, Zach, Kierra, and myself all sat around the room, along with several other members of the security team.

"I ASKED YOU A QUESTION." Bruce barked.

"We're just trying to help," I mumbled.

"WELL STOP!" he shouted. "You are NOT security, do you understand? Not in any way, shape, or form—"

"We're truly sorry for the intrusion," Zach spoke calmly. "It won't happen again."

Finally, Bruce's face seemed to drop one shade of purple. "Good."

Everyone went quiet for a moment, and then I was surprised to hear Noah speak up.

"From a purely *non*-security standpoint, I think it's a little odd that the video cut out exactly when the incident occurred." Before Bruce could start shouting again, Noah quickly continued: "Again, this has *nothing* do with security, and more just a general observation — as a person."

Bruce glared at him. "We've reviewed the footage in question and found no abnormalities."

"How?" I spoke up. I couldn't help myself. "It literally goes blank the same hour she was attacked!"

Zach spoke over me. "I think what my colleague is trying to say is that the video could be really helpful in tracking down the culprit. So maybe if we just took a second look at the footage—"

Bruce smacked his desk. "YOU. ARE. NOT. SECURITY."

"Right, of course," Zach said quickly. "Sorry."

I shook my head. Why was Zach being so flimsy with this case?

"Now. Your assistance will no longer be required for this case," said Bruce. "We found semen on the victim, and we have Rapid DNA testing here on the island — thanks to Rocky."

Zach's eyes went wide. "You — you found semen?"

"That's right."

"Well, what are you planning to compare it with?" I asked. "I'm assuming you don't have DNA samples of everyone on this island."

He glared at me. "We've had an open channel with the FBI since the plague scare. They've agreed to run it through their criminal offenders database. We're expecting to hear back from them any minute now."

"The FBI?" Zach looked like he had seen a ghost. What was going on with him?

I bit my lip, annoyed that we were being shut out from the investigation.

"What about the victim?" I challenged. "I'd like to speak with Ethyl too."

"The victim is in a state of shock."

"Right…" I said. "That's where *therapy* could be helpful."

"Elliot—"

"No!" I spoke over Zach, blood boiling. "What the fuck is wrong with everyone? The video was obviously tampered with, and they won't even let us talk to the victim. This is a fucking coverup, and Officer Cholesterol is involved—"

"GET OUT!" Bruce jumped up and knocked over a chair. "OUT OF MY OFFICE. NOW!"

Zach sighed and gave me a tired look.

"What the hell is that guy's problem?" I fumed as we walked downstairs.

"I thought he seemed pleasant," said Kierra.

"Listen," said Zach. "We might not like him, but we have to play nice with him. And he's actually right about one thing, Elliot. You can't just go around making accusations without evidence."

"The evidence was erased!" I said, exasperated. "Jesus, Zach. Why are you being such a coward tonight? It's like you don't even want the case to be solved."

"Hey, that's not fair," he said. "We're all working hard on this."

"Yeah," Kierra chimed in. "I can't believe I put out like that, just for you to waste it all with another temper tantrum."

"Does anyone even want me here?" I snapped.

"I do!" Noah shot his hand in the air. "I think you're doing great."

"Fantastic," I grumbled. "I need to talk with Rocky again. We're obviously missing something here."

"Well, there's no way they're going to allow that after your little performance in there," said Zach.

"I get it!" I said. "I fucked up, okay? Can we let it go?"

"No, I don't think we can," said Kierra. "Raise your hand if you think Dr. Harper is ruining everything."

Noah eagerly raised his hand again.

"There it is," said Kierra.

I stared at Noah incredulously.

"Oh, wait—" He dropped his hand. Then he frowned. "Sorry, can you repeat the question?"

Before we could continue bickering, there was a sudden commotion in the stairwell behind us.

"STOP!"

I spun around, surprised to see five guards sprinting toward us — led by Bruce.

"Zach Johnson!" he shouted.

Zach's eyes went wide, like a deer in headlights.

And then, to my absolute horror, they tackled my best friend to the ground and cuffed his hands behind his back.

"By order of the FBI, you are hereby under arrest for the rape of Ethyl McDougal."

PART THREE

"LET ME TALK TO HIM!" I shouted. "He has a CONSTITUTIONAL RIGHT to legal counsel."

"You're not a lawyer—"

"Well, I'm representing him while we wait for one."

"That's not — that's not how it works."

"Are you sure about that?" I asked. "Because if you're wrong and you deny him his rights, the entire case will be thrown out."

The truth was, I had no idea what I was talking about. I was desperate, and at this point, I was just tossing out threats in hopes that one of them would stick.

Bruce studied me for a moment and shook his head.

"Why are you defending this guy anyway?"

"He's my best friend," I said. "And he didn't do this."

"Did your *best friend* tell you why his DNA is in a criminal database?"

I bit my lip. "No."

"Well…" Bruce grabbed a key from his belt and walked over to unlock the door. "You might want to ask him about that. And keep it quick in there. Big storm about to hit the island."

He stepped aside to let me into the tiny, dark room. I hurried past him and shut the door behind me — finally alone with my friend.

"What the FUCK, Zach?" I stormed up to him.

"I didn't do it," he said quietly.

"I know that," I snapped. "So why the *fuck* was your semen on an old woman?"

"I don't know."

I started pacing around him. "Have you had sex with anyone

111

on this island?"

"No."

"Have you masturbated since we got here?"

Zach stared at me. "Elliot."

"Answer the question!"

"No," he said. "No, okay? We've been pretty busy."

"Then where the hell did your sperm come from, Zach!"

"I don't *know*."

I threw my hands in the air. "You have to help me out here. Because right now your best defense is magical teleporting jizz."

He slammed his fists onto the table with uncharacteristic frustration. "What do you want me to say!?"

"I don't know, Zach..." I glowered. "Maybe you could start by explaining why your DNA is in a *criminal database*."

His face went dark.

"It's nothing."

I stepped closer to him. "Zach, remember when I was in prison and you helped me?"

He grunted.

"Well, now you're in a tough spot and I'm here to help you," I said. "But I can't do that if you're not honest with me."

He took a deep breath and let out a loud sigh.

"It was back in college," he began. "I was coming home from a party around midnight — alone. I saw a girl screaming and running through the quad. Before I could ask if she was okay, police surrounded me and beat me to a pulp."

"What? Why?"

"Why do you think, Elliot?" he said. "Look at me."

"What about you?"

"Christ, you can be dense," he said. "Look at the *color of my skin*."

"But you didn't do anything!"

"I was a black man on campus when a white girl got raped."

"But—" It still didn't make sense to me, so I repeated myself. "You didn't *do* anything!"

"It doesn't matter!" he said. "Have you ever been pulled over for no reason? Or tailed the entire time you're shopping for clothes? Or reported for walking through a nice neighborhood?"

"No…"

"Right, you're innocent until proven guilty" he said. "It's the opposite for me. Why do you think I'm so calm and reserved all the time? It's not that I don't get passionate like you. I'm just… afraid of expressing it."

"That's not fair!"

"Yeah, I'm aware of that." He rolled his eyes. "My point is that guilt and innocence don't matter as much in cases like mine."

"But you *were* proven innocent, weren't you?" I asked. "They tested your DNA, right?"

"It was inconclusive," he said. "But they still brought it to trial, so I had to fight it. I lost everything — Friends… Scholarship… I went bankrupt."

I shook my head in disbelief. I couldn't believe I missed this entire period of his life.

"Why didn't you ever tell me this?" I asked quietly.

He looked down. "Because I didn't want you to think of me as a… possible rapist."

It pained me that he could ever imagine I would think that. But based on everything I was learning about him tonight, I was starting to understand why he was afraid of reaching out.

There was a gentle rumble of thunder in the distance as I stepped to his side and put my arm around his shoulder.

"You're not fighting alone this time."

I've never asked Siri to FaceTime a convicted rapist before, but hey — desperate times call for desperate measures.

"Do you really think this is a good idea?" asked Zach as the ringtone chimed.

"I don't know," I said honestly. "But I can't think of any other options."

I was surprised to see the screen flicker to indicate a successful connection.

"Hello?"

"Paul," I said quickly. "Thank you for taking my call."

I was surprised to see another young black man appear on the screen, with huge bags under his eyes.

"I'm sorry, who are you?"

"My name is Dr. Harper," I said. "I'm a therapist, and I'm looking into a rape."

Paul's eyes went into a frenzied panic. "I didn't do anything! I swear to god, I've been in my house all night, you can check my tracker—"

"No," I said. "Don't worry. You're not a suspect. We're hundreds of miles away from you."

He let out a huge sigh of relief and his shoulders relaxed.

"Oh, thank god." Then he frowned. "So... why are you calling me?"

"Because both of our cases involve an elderly woman and a man named Rocky."

"I never touched my grandma," he said, breaking into tears. "I never touched her. Dr. Harper, I've never hurt anyone, let alone—"

"I believe you."

He raised his eyebrows and sniffled. "You — what?"

I was pretty sure he hadn't heard those words in a very long time.

"My friend is being accused of the same thing, and I know for a fact that he didn't do this," I said. "But like you, his semen was found at the scene of the crime."

"Oh my god," he said. "It's happening again!"

"Yes," I said. "We don't have much time, and I need your help."

He nodded urgently and sat up. "Whatever you need."

"After sexual activity, how do you dispose of your..."

"The trash," he said, leaning into the camera. "You know, I've thought about this a million times. I was thinking it could be a garbage man?"

I sighed. "That doesn't fit. It would have been dried and contaminated. That would have shown up on the test."

"What about an ex-girlfriend?" he asked hopefully. "What if she... saved it?"

"Tell me the names of your exes."

He rattled off a few names and I looked at Zach for confirmation.

He shook his head four times.

"That's not it," I said. "Paul, I really need you to think here. And I'm not judging any kinky stuff, okay? Is there *any* other way that someone could have fresh samples of your sperm?"

Paul bit down on his lip like he was thinking hard.

"N — No..." he said, shaking his head. "I'm sorry."

I turned to Zach with an apologetic look. He shrugged, like he had already accepted his fate.

"Wait a minute!"

I turned back to the screen. "What?"

"It was forever ago, but... I was a sperm donor."

I spun around. "ZACH, HAVE YOU EVER—"

"Yes." He bolted upright. "I needed money after high school. But Elliot — that was ages ago."

"Frozen sperm can survive for decades," I said, shoving the phone at Zach. "Keep talking with him."

"Wait, where are you going?" he asked.

"Rocky's room." I ran to the door. "There's one more piece to this puzzle."

I dropped the dildo on the desk.

"START TALKING."

Rocky looked up at me curiously. "Is that a...?"

"The jig is up," I said. "I know about the sperm donors and your fake penis."

He raised his eyebrows. "What in the world are you talking about, Doctor?"

"STOP PLAYING STUPID WITH ME." I flipped over the desk. "You're raping these women and planting DNA evidence."

He gave me an incredulous look. "Do I need to show you my dick again?"

"You're not using your dick." I pointed at the sex toy on the ground. "You're using THAT."

"What?" He snorted. "What pleasure would a rapist get from using a dildo?"

"Rape isn't about pleasure," I hissed. "It's about power. Do you feel powerful, Rocky? Attacking elderly women with sex toys?"

"You're insane."

"Am I?" I grabbed the dildo and chucked it at his face. "Because from where I'm sitting, you're the insane one. You've built this entire platform around being the 'victim', and you know what's scary? I think you're actually starting to believe it."

"I *am* the victim."

"NO!" I barked. "The victims are the ones you violate and terrorize. The ones who live in trauma and constant fear of it happening again. The ones who blame themselves when they did nothing wrong. The ones who have to replay your horror, over and over again."

"I was burned alive!" he shouted, finally getting heated.

Good. Now all I had to do was keep provoking him.

"You know what's funny, Rocky?" I said, channeling what I imagined his father sounded like. "Standing here across from you, I can see just how powerless you really are. Weak and impotent. Like a sniveling little bitch. It's no wonder you can't find a woman your own age—"

He grabbed the dildo from the floor and lunged at me. "FUCK YOU!"

I continued as he tackled me. "Small, pathetic, unlovable—"

He shoved the dildo down my throat.

"I'LL FUCKING CHOKE YOU, JUST LIKE I DID WITH THOSE GRANNY BITCHES."

And that was all we needed.

The door burst open and Bruce came sprinting in with the rest of the team. They pulled Rocky off me and forced him into handcuffs.

"YOU'VE GOT ABSOLUTELY NOTHING ON ME!" he spat as they dragged him away. "YOU HAVE NO EVIDENCE. YOU THINK ANYONE'S GONNA BELIEVE A NI—"

Bruce thankfully elbowed him in the face before he could finish that word.

Then to my surprise, Bruce came back and helped me up from the ground. "You alright?"

"Mmf—mmmmff—" I pulled the dildo out of my mouth and gave him a big grin. "I told you we would get a confession."

He stared at me for a second and shook his head.

"You're a fuckin' weirdo."

"I've never been on the receiving end of your sessions before," said Zach. "It's pretty... intense."

"I'm sorry I shouted..."

Zach laughed. "Are you kidding? After all these years, I'd be more concerned if you *weren't* shouting."

I smiled sheepishly and tapped my foot against the ground.

"Seriously though," he said. "Thanks for everything"

"Don't thank me yet," I said. "We're not completely out of the woodwork. Rocky really covered his tracks. We still haven't found your sperm samples or his sex toy — we had to use Kierra's to provoke him."

"I still can't believe he planned all this out..." said Zach, shaking his head in disbelief. "I mean, he knew my entire past — he knew I'd be an easy scapegoat, and he knew I'd be on the island. Christ, he even convinced the festival to have Rapid DNA tests so they could instantly clear his name."

"That's what why we *need* his confession on record," I said. "Without it, you're the top suspect."

"What about the security footage?" asked Zach. "Did they ever recover it — or figure out who deleted it?"

"It was all Rocky," I said. "He had security key access because he was a firefighter. Bruce is revising their protocols now, but it won't matter. The footage is gone."

Zach nodded. "So I guess I'll be locked in here for the rest of the trip…"

"As soon as Rocky confesses on tape, you'll be out of here."

Zach gave me a sad smile, like he had already been defeated.

"Hey…" I walked closer to him. "Come on. This isn't going to be like last time. This time, it's a happy ending."

He smiled again, but his eyes weren't smiling at all. There was a tiredness deep within him that I hadn't really noticed before.

We sat there for a while in silence. I decided that I would stay here with him until the confession came. He wasn't going to spend another second on his own. We would wait out the coming storm together.

But suddenly we heard shouting outside, and then the door burst open.

"Rocky's dead!" Bruce's eyes were wide.

"WHAT?" I stormed up to him, heart racing. "What do you mean he's *dead?*"

"Hung himself," he said, panting. "Used his own fucking shirt."

"HOW THE FUCK COULD YOU LET THIS HAPPEN?"

An agonizing sensation of dread exploded inside of me.

"There's something else…" said Bruce, looking down. "We have to send Zach home."

I did a double-take. "Home?"

"The FBI is taking over his case," said Bruce. "We couldn't get Rocky's confession on tape, and now he's gone—"

"You're sending away an innocent man?" I hissed. "You heard his confession yourself!"

"Well the FBI didn't," said Bruce, walking over to Zach with a pair of handcuffs. "I'm sure they'll figure things out."

"GET OFF HIM!" I lunged at Bruce, but I was no match for him. He flicked me aside like a fly.

Zach didn't put up a fight. He hung his head as the handcuffs clicked around his wrists.

"Zach!" I ran up to him and grabbed his arm.

Bruce looked at us for a second and nodded, at least having the decency to let us say goodbye.

"It's okay," said Zach calmly. "I'll be okay."

"I'm so sorry," I stammered. "I failed you."

"You did everything you could, Elliot..." he said. "Happy endings are just a bit more... complicated for some of us."

"I'm coming with you," I said decisively. "We'll go home and fight this."

"No." He shook his head. "You need to stay here."

"Why!"

"Because this island needs you," he said. "There's a storm coming, and you know I'm not talking about the weather."

With that, Bruce walked him out the door and escorted him to the airstrip, where a plane would soon take him far, far away from us.

"What's going on!"

Noah and Kierra hurried up to me.

"Rocky killed himself," I said, swallowing. "They're taking Zach home for questioning."

"Oh no!" said Noah. "Is there anything we can do?"

"No." I shook my head. "We need to stick together now, okay? All we have is each other."

The two of them nodded solemnly. Kierra didn't even crack a joke.

Noah rubbed my back gently, which made my eyes sting as I tried to hold back tears. Without Zach around, I needed to be strong for them. He wanted us to stay here and help, and that's exactly what I intended to do.

As the three of us walked back to our rooms along the shadowy jungle trails, a bolt of lightning cracked through the sky and unleashed a torrent of rain on the island.

The storm was here.

End of Patient File: UnCanceled4Victims

Our Fifth Date

With the storm raging outside, I decided to keep things simple tonight.

Popcorn — kettle corn, extra butter, low calorie, and regular — I wasn't sure if he had a preference. Plus eighteen potential movie choices in my queue, with at least one film in every genre, but we could keep searching if he didn't like any of them. Oh, and a few different types of soda, like diet and orange and vanilla, and some without caffeine in case he was sensitive to caffeine.

Just a totally normal, simple movie night.

"Oh, shoot!"

My heart sank as I realized I forgot to grab candy from the gift shop. But that was okay! I still had enough time to run over.

Knock knock.

I raised my eyebrows. Doc was early.

I hurried over to the door to let him in. But it wasn't Doc.

"I'm bored."

Kierra pushed past me and let herself inside.

"Oh, hey Kierra!" I said, trailing after her. "Um, listen, I'm actually having a movie night with Doc."

"Perfect." She sat down on the couch and took a handful of popcorn. "What are we watching?"

I swallowed nervously.

"Well, actually... We were kind of hoping to... Do something private."

"Gross!" Kierra spat out some popcorn. "You're gonna bonk the doc?"

"No!" I protested. "Just — kiss."

"Still disgusting." She reached for more popcorn. "Just so you know, I don't approve of your lifestyle."

"Kierra, that's really homophobic."

"Oh, I have nothing against the gays," she said. "It's your lifestyle choice of Dr. Harper that I don't approve of."

I sighed. "I really like him."

"Ugh, why? He sucks!"

"He does not!" I said defensively. "He cares so much about other people. He's really passionate and empathetic. And I think he's starting to open up his heart to me!"

Kierra gave me a funny look. "I think you've still got some Ambien in your system, because you're not describing any Dr. Harper that I know."

"I know you guys don't get along—"

"He kidnapped me and locked me in his garage."

"You did the same thing to me!" I said. "But people can change. Kierra, I brought you here because I trust you. And you *know* why I trust you."

She glowered. "You swear you haven't told him, right?"

"No, I promise!" I said truthfully. "But my point is, I trust Doc just like I trust you. And if you just give him a chance—"

"Trust me with what?"

Doc entered the room with some chips and ice cream.

"Nothing!" I said, jumping up. "Kierra was just about

to leave—"

"Actually, I think I'll stay," she drawled from the couch. "Not much else to do in a storm. Thanks for letting me crash with you, boys."

I felt my face flush with irritation. Doc and I were never going to get a chance to kiss on this island.

"Noah...?" Doc glared at me.

"*Sorry*," I mouthed.

He took a deep breath and wandered over to the couch.

"Can you at least scooch over?"

"No, I already claimed middle seat," said Kierra. "Best view of the TV. So, what are we watching?"

As Doc reluctantly took a seat to her left, I sulked over to the couch and sat on her other side.

"Oh this is fun," she said, wrapping her arms around us. "Date night with my ex husband and his hideously deformed boyfriend."

"Kierra!"

Needless to say, the rest of the night did not go well. Kierra decided that we should watch *Saw III* and laughed through the entire thing. Every time she made a comment, I could see Doc's mood getting worse.

"I don't think it's very realistic," said Kierra through a mouthful of chips. "Blood doesn't actually spray like that in real life."

Doc sighed loudly. "Because you've seen someone's head get blown off by a *shotgun collar* in real life?"

"I've seen a lot of things," said Kierra. "You were my first dick burner though."

"Jesus Christ, would you shut the fuck up and let us watch this godawful movie that YOU PICKED—"

"Hey, Doc!" I said hurriedly. "Can you help me in the

kitchen for a second?"

"Spoiler alert!" Kierra called as we stood up. "He's going to try to kiss you."

My face went red again as we made our way into the kitchen.

"Doc..." I began.

"It's not your fault, Noah."

"Still, I feel awful," I said. "This is the worst date ever."

"Hey, it's not all bad," he said with a smile. "You made some really good popcorn."

I let out a small laugh. "I'm glad you like it — but you don't have to stay if you don't want."

"Are you kidding?" he said encouragingly. "I'm not leaving tonight without getting the next key."

"Oh!" I said. "I totally forgot about that. The fifth key is faith!"

Doc raised his eyebrows. "You're spiritual?"

"Sort of," I said. "It doesn't have to be a specific religion or anything. Could be God, angels, the universe, divine energy, or even human connection. Just something bigger than us. Then we can get out of our heads and stop trying to control everything."

"That's so cool," said Doc with a nod. "I couldn't agree more. Hey, do you want to stay in here for a bit and keep talking about this?"

"Sure!" I said, pulling out two chairs. "I think Kierra can entertain herself. By the way, about what she said—"

"It's okay," he said, looking down nervously. "For what it's worth, I was sort of hoping we'd... kiss too."

My heart lit up, and then I realized that I couldn't wait anymore.

I didn't care that this was our worst date yet. I didn't care that Kierra was in the other room. I didn't care that every single detail of the night was wrong.

All I wanted to do was kiss him.

So I took a deep breath and softened my lips.

But I didn't make it very far before we were once again interrupted.

"HEY!" Kierra stood in the doorway, arms crossed. "Pay attention to me."

Ghost Story

PART ONE

"Unimaginable pain and trauma..."

I looked at the self-proclaimed 'bridge to all beings' and couldn't shake the image of Professor Trelawney from *Harry Potter*. Unruly hair, hippy clothing, and thick glasses that made her eyes bulge like an insect.

It didn't help that her name was Aurora. Aurora Borealis.

No, I'm not kidding. I wish I was.

"Uh, yeah," I said. "Listen, the security folks wanted me to talk with you. Something about a missing woman?"

"A *dead* woman," Aurora corrected me. "She wishes to speak with you."

"Of course she does..." I grumbled.

I like to think I'm open-minded with patients, but the supernatural has always been a sore subject with me. I just... I can't stand that shit. There are contests out there offering millions of dollars to anyone who can demonstrate supernatural abilities in a controlled environment, and — surprise, surprise — the prizes remain unclaimed.

"You don't trust the spiritual realm..." She peered at me through her ridiculous glasses.

Lightning and thunder cracked from the storm outside.

"I'm actually a spiritual man myself," I said. "But no, I don't believe anyone has the power to predict the future or communicate with dead people."

"Well, I wouldn't call it prediction or communication," she said. "It's more about allowing the universe to flow through us, so that we can feel all of its truths."

I let out a sigh and glared at her.

"And you... Elliot Harper... I feel death around you..."

"What is that supposed to mean?" I said defensively.

"Two young men..." She closed her eyes. "High school boys. Lost their lives to gun violence. I see one of them bleeding on top of you. So young... So young..."

I suddenly felt a surge of dread and anxiety in my stomach. Alex and Ian. How the hell did she know that?

But then my logical brain took over, and I let out a small laugh.

Of course.

"The details of that shooting were made public in my trial," I said confidently. "Anyone can find it on Google."

"And a young inmate who died in your arms..." she continued as if I hadn't spoken. "I sense only gratitude and hope in his spirit."

"Sam..." I muttered under my breath. "That's all public record too."

"But there's someone else, isn't there...?" she said gravely. "In this spirit, I sense endless darkness."

I thought for a moment, and then remembered... Dr. Zhang.

"You definitely got that one right," I said. "But again, that was all over the national news. You don't exactly need to channel the spirit world for that."

She gave me an all-knowing smile, which only pissed me off more.

"What?" I snapped.

"Elliot Harper, do you think I am trying to impress or persuade you with this information?" She tilted her head. "No... No... I'm simply trying to understand..."

"Understand what?" I said impatiently.

"Why she chose you..."

"Why *who* chose me?" I said.

"Unimaginable pain and trauma..." she said again, closing her eyes. "Suffering beyond comprehension."

"Look, I'm going to be honest with you." I closed my notebook. "The only reason the security team sent you here is because they're desperate, okay? They've messed up so many times that they can't afford to dismiss any leads. But this — the whole psychic act? It's a waste of our time. Not a single person has died on this island since the festival began."

"I understand," she said, standing up. "I'm very sorry for bothering you, Elliot Harper."

Even when she was polite, everything about Aurora annoyed me.

I walked her out of my office, eager to be finished with this session.

We stood together in the doorway for an uncomfortably long time, until I noticed she was crying.

"I'm sorry for being short with you," I said. "We just have a lot of—"

"I weep not for myself," she said. "I weep for her."

I took a deep breath, trying to conceal my frustration.

"Listen, if I could help, I would."

"Her spirit is in agony," continued Aurora, tears now streaming freely down her face. "She cannot pass through the gates of heaven until you hear her message."

"Okay, let's hear it then."

Aurora leaned in close to my ear, and then she let out a bloodcurdling shriek. I jumped up and slammed my head into the door frame.

"UNIMAGINABLE PAIN AND TRAUMA!" she screamed. "SUFFERING BEYOND COMPREHENSION!"

"Jesus fucking Christ!" I shouted back, massaging my forehead. "Get the fuck out of here!"

"PAIN! TRAUMA! SUFFERING!" She wailed as she stumbled out of the building, arms flailing above her head. Her voice continued to echo as the door slammed shut behind her.

I opened up the mini-fridge to grab some ice and held it to my head. Then I dug through the shelves behind the mirror in search of Advil. I wasn't even sure if the throbbing in my head was from the door frame or from Aurora's screaming.

Why the hell did the security team send her to me? She was obviously unstable, and she had used every psychic trick in the book to gather information about me before our meeting.

Nobody on the island was dead.

Nobody was even missing.

So *why* did they send her to me?

I took out my phone and decided to give Aurora a taste of her own cyber-stalking medicine. I googled her name with 'bridge to all beings' and instantly found her on Instagram, Facebook, YouTube, and Twitter.

Her website was filled with endless snake-oil offers, such as:

Have you lost a loved one? Aurora Borealis is here to help you find them. Only $170!

30 minute Aura Cleansing with Aurora — now only $85!

Aurora Borealis reunites mother with deceased child on Good Morning America

I closed the website in disgust. *This* is why I hated the supernatural. It was just a bunch of opportunistic con-artists taking advantage of vulnerable—

Before I could finish my internal soap box monologue, the door swung open. I was half expecting Aurora to come marching back in with a bill for my psychic reading.

Instead, I was surprised to see Noah standing in the doorway, soaking wet.

"Noah?" I raised my eyebrows. "Our date isn't until tonight, right?"

"Doc," he said, out of breath. "Something happened to Kierra."

PART TWO

"What are you talking about?" I asked. "What happened to her?"

"She's missing!" he said. "I can't find her anywhere."

To be honest, I normally wouldn't care if Kierra went missing. But I didn't trust her for a second, and I certainly didn't trust her being out of our sight.

"Doc? Did you hear what I said?"

"Yeah," I said. "Sorry — so, what makes you think she's missing?"

"She isn't answering her phone. It's not even showing up on the Find My iPhone map that Zach set up."

"Noah, she could have just turned her phone off."

"I don't think so!" he said. "She never misses breakfast with me. We have a morning check-in."

I raised my eyebrows. "For what?"

"It doesn't matter," he said quickly. "Doc, you have to trust me. Something happened to her."

"She's probably just in her room."

"I checked her room!" he said. "I've checked everywhere. Please, you have to help me."

I sighed. "Noah, it's pouring outside."

He gave me an angry look and crossed his arms.

"Fine," I said, grabbing my coat. "Let's go."

We hurried down the hall and out into the storm, only to find Aurora sitting cross-legged in the pouring rain.

"*Unimaginable pain and trauma...*" she murmured to herself, rocking back and forth. "*Suffering beyond comprehension...*"

"Are you okay?" asked Noah gently.

"Just leave her," I said. "She's a psychic fraud named Aurora Borealis. She was in my office earlier, ranting about a dead woman."

Noah's eyes went wide. "Oh my god, you don't think...?"

"No!" I said. "For Christ's sake, Noah."

"What if she can help us!" Noah protested. He knelt down next to Aurora. "Excuse me, will you please help us find our missing friend?"

Her eyes went wide. "You... Sweet boy... You must also hear her message."

"Okay!" said Noah, leaning closer to her. "I'm ready."

"Noah, don't!"

But he shushed me, so I backed away and braced for the inevitable...

"UNIMAGINABLE PAIN AND TRAUMA!" she screamed into his ear. "SUFFERING BEYOND COMPREHENSION!"

Noah jumped back, terrified.

"Told you," I grumbled.

"Oh my gosh..." said Noah, gazing back at Aurora. "Kierra experienced pain and suffering."

"No," I said. "She *causes* pain and suffering."

"I'm serious, Doc!" he said. "There's a lot of stuff you don't know about her childhood."

"Like what?" I scoffed.

"She was kidnapped from her parents and brainwashed by a cult!" he said. "Aurora must know all about that. She needs to come with us."

"Aurora is spouting off Barnum statements that could apply to anyone!" I said, exasperated. "Every adult human has experienced some sort of pain or suffering or trauma."

"BEYOND COMPREHENSION!" Aurora wailed.

"Please, come with us," said Noah. "Help us find our friend, Kierra."

Aurora nodded dramatically and stumbled up to join us.

"Handsome boys..." she said as we started walking. "The ghost has chosen two handsome boys to share such suffering..."

"Would you shut up already?" I snapped. "You're about to

meet a new ghost when I shoot myself."

"So I've already checked the east and south sides of the island," said Noah through the strong winds. "Do you think we should try north or west next?"

Aurora threw her hands into the sky at the exact moment a bolt of lightning came piercing down.

Dumb luck.

"NORTH, SWEET BOY!"

And so we traveled north, battered and soaked by the storm.

"Do you really think Kierra is dead?" Noah asked Aurora.

"Sweet boy…" she began. "There is only so much suffering one can endure before the heart inevitably falters. But do not fear. The universe claims all its children back with infinite love."

"But we were making so much progress!" said Noah.

"What progress?" I said. "Noah, why did you bring Kierra to this island?"

We looked at each other for a moment. I could see in his eyes that he wanted to tell me. But he shook his head.

"I can't tell you, Doc. She made me promise. But you trust me, right?"

"I trust you!" I said. "I don't trust Kierra."

"UNIMAGINABLE PAIN AND TRAUMA!" Aurora shrieked. "SUFFERING BEYOND COMPREHENSION!"

"Oh my god." I rubbed my eyes. "Let's keep moving."

The next ten minutes continued in peaceful silence, until Aurora decided to speak again.

"You lost your father."

I turned to face her. "Congratulations on your ability to read obituaries."

"But you lost him long before death, didn't you?"

I bit my lip hard, unable to tame my burning hatred for this woman.

"Again, that statement could apply to anyone."

"He would like to share a message with you…"

"Let me guess," I said, getting up in her face. "UNIMAGINABLE PAIN AND TRUAMA."

"No…" she said, unfazed by my shouting. "He is sorry. So

very sorry…"

"Sorry for what?" I asked. "Instead of vague statements, give me some *actual* details that only the ghost of my father would know."

"When he left you, he also left behind a very deep and painful wound…" She bowed her head, and I felt an old pressure built up inside of me. "A wound that makes it quite difficult to become close with others… You interpreted his rejection as proof of your own defectiveness."

"Shut up," I said quietly.

"But it was he who was defective…" she continued. "Your wound was formed from a false conclusion."

"Shut… up…"

"And now he wishes for you to let go of that wound…"

"FAT LOT OF GOOD THAT DOES ME NOW, YOU FUCKING COWARD!" I screamed at him — or her. "WHERE THE FUCK WERE YOU WHEN YOU LEFT A FUCKING CHILD TO TAKE CARE OF YOUR WIFE?"

Noah's eyes went wide, and even Aurora looked surprised by my reaction.

My shoulders moved up and down with every shallow breath.

Jesus Christ, I was losing it out here.

Had I seriously just let myself get provoked by a goddamn psychic medium?

"Well, I'd recognize that shouting anywhere…" came a familiar voice.

We all looked up in shock to see Kierra stepping out from the mist.

She was standing in front of Linus's germ fortress.

"What the hell are you doing out here?" I demanded.

"Nice to see you too…" said Kierra. "I was out for a walk and got caught in the rain. Decided to take shelter outside our old stomping ground. The roof juts out just enough—"

I walked past her and approached the front door of the fortress, but I couldn't remember the code to get in. The sticky note from Linus was all the way back in my room.

"Bullshit." I turned around. "You decided to take a stroll in the middle of the storm?"

"Weather changes." She shrugged. "Anywho... What's with Miss Frizzle?"

"This is Aurora Borealis!" said Noah. "She helped us find you."

"Aurora... Borealias?" Kierra broke into a smirk. "Ah, that explains Dr. Harper's mood."

"Indeed..." Aurora nodded gravely. "I sensed your presence in the north."

"You said she was *dead*," I snapped.

"Oh, this is not the suffering spirit." Aurora pointed at Kierra. "No... No... The spirit came from much further away — across the ocean it seems. And the spirit is still with us... Oh yes... Still with us indeed..."

"How convenient," I said skeptically. "Your prediction changes the moment we receive new information."

"UNIMAGINABLE PAIN AND TRAUMA!" she cried, falling to the ground. "SUFFERING BEYOND COMPREHENSION!"

"Yikes." Kierra raised her eyebrows. "Sounds like me when the pool bar closes."

I rolled my eyes, but before I could walk away from them, Aurora added a new line:

"A MOTHER'S WORST NIGHTMARE."

I froze — paralyzed by the hysterical sobbing that suddenly sounded so familiar.

I knew that cry.

Mom?

PART THREE

When we got back to the room, I locked myself in the bedroom and called my mom's phone.

It rang twice, then—

"Elliot?"

I let out a sigh of relief when she picked up on the third ring.

"Mom! Hi, how are you?"

"I'm fine," she said. "Is everything okay?"

"Yes, all good," I said. "You're in good health, right? No pain or illness?"

"No... Elliot, what in the world is going on?"

"Thanks mom!" I said. "Gotta go."

I hung up the phone and rushed into the living room.

"Wrong again!" I said triumphantly. "My mom is perfectly fine. Just talked with her on the phone."

Aurora glanced at me with an all-knowing smile. "It was not me who declared your mother dead... No... I believe that was you."

"But you would have taken credit for it if it was true!" I said. "You just keep making up predictions so you can claim you're right whenever one comes true. Well so far you're 0 for 2."

"While you keep score, the spirit suffers..." she moaned. "Please, won't you hear her message?"

"Of course we will!" Noah chimed in.

"No — Noah, it's just more screaming about pain and trauma."

"But have you heard the *whole* message yet?" he asked.

"We don't need to!" I threw my hands in the air. "Kierra is fine. My mom is fine. What other dead woman do you know who would haunt us?"

"Please tell us your message," said Noah, closing his eyes. "We are ready to receive it."

Jesus Christ. For once, I actually wished Kierra was here to make her snide comments.

"You must both be ready..." Aurora looked at me. "One resists."

"Doc, please!" Noah scooched closer to me. "Can you do this for me?"

I sighed and shook my head. "Okay. Fine. Let's hear the message."

Aurora nodded darkly and took a deep breath, closing her eyes.

"HELP HIM, ELLIOT HARPER!" She lunged at me and shook my arms. "HE HAS SURVIVED UNIMAGINABLE PAIN AND TRAUMA! HE HAS EXPERIENCED SUFFERING BEYOND COMPREHENSION. AND NOW, A CHILD WITH NO HOME AND NO FAMILY... IT IS A MOTHER'S WORST NIGHTMARE. PLEASE, I BEG OF YOU. HELP HIM!"

I struggled to back away from her. "Get away from me!"

"HELP HIM, ELLIOT HARPER!" she pleaded, grabbing at my shirt. "I BEG OF YOU!"

"You're fucking crazy." I escaped her grasp and ran to the other side of the couch. "Noah, she's all yours. I'm going back to my room."

"I am trying to guide you to your destiny!" Aurora called as I ran into my room. "Why do you resist your destiny?"

I slammed the door shut behind me.

An hour later, there was a knock at my door.

I peered out to make sure it wasn't Aurora. But thankfully she was at a safe distance, sitting across the table from Noah playing cards.

"Good afternoon, Elliot." Bruce stepped inside. "I've got

what you asked for."

He dropped a huge stack of papers on my desk — almost as thick as a book.

"That's everything?"

"Every website, social media profile, search history, and stream that Aurora has visited on this island," he said. "Every request goes through our network, and VPNs aren't allowed."

"Perfect," I said. "Thanks so much."

"That's a shitload of internet activity for such a short period of time," he said. "Even for a social media influencer. You need us to investigate anything from our end?"

"Actually," I said. "There is one thing you could do."

"Sure thing."

Bruce had gotten a lot nicer since he took Zach away from us.

"Can you check out that fortress where Linus Solomon was staying?" I asked, handing him the sticky note. "Here's the entrance code."

He raised his eyebrows. "Any particular reason?"

"I just... I have a feeling."

"I hate when you get those," said Bruce. "I'll check it out."

"Thanks," I said.

He walked out of the room, and I returned to my desk. I felt a surge of relief looking at the stack of papers. This was going to confirm everything I knew about Aurora. She was a fraud like all of the other mediums, but she did have one unique ability — she had mastered the art of cyber-stalking. She used social media, news stories, and archives to create a sense of omnipotence.

Now all I had to do was prove my theory.

I reached forward to start with page one, but I was immediately interrupted by the sound of my phone buzzing.

I answered the anonymous call. "Hello?"

"Is this Elliot Harper?" said the voice.

"Yes, who am I speaking to?"

"My name is Walter Field, with Field and Fisher. I represent the estate of Gina Turnmore. I'm sorry to call with such bleak news."

"Wait a minute — who?"

"Ms. Turnmore passed away last night in a car crash," he said. "You're listed as the sole beneficiary to her estate."

"I think you have the wrong Elliot Harper," I said. " I don't know anyone by that name."

"Hmm… Are you sure?" he asked. "She even listed you as the child's legal guardian. She was quite specific about it, actually. She wrote here that you were the only one she trusted with her son. Said you saved him when everyone else failed."

"Wait a minute," I said. "Her son?"

"Yes," he said. "The boy's name is James."

After the call ended, I fell to the ground in physical pain.

It felt like I was having a heart attack.

James, the traumatized young boy who Noah and I met at the beach… The boy who was sold into sex trafficking… The boy who watched his friends get burned alive… The boy who endured years of psychological and physical torment… The boy who had only just returned to his mother months ago…

And now… He lost his last remaining parent to a car crash? It couldn't be possible.

My chest burned at the injustice of it all. It wasn't fair. It wasn't possible that the world could be so cruel to one human being. A fucking child.

Looking back up at the stack of papers on my desk, I wondered how Aurora knew.

Presumably, Gina's obituary would be somewhere in there. Along with some news articles about my connection with James. Maybe she called the family lawyer and dug up information about Gina's will.

But there was one thing that really confused me… Aurora wasn't asking me for money or internet fame. No, she actually seemed to be guided by this idea that she was helping people to follow their destiny. She wanted me to help James. She wanted me to forgive my father.

Those weren't selfish things.

She was using research to implement the will of the universe — or at least, her interpretation of it.

And in a way, that's exactly what I sought out to do with my patients.

I had a strong feeling that I knew what was in those papers. But in the end, did it really matter? There were much bigger things at stake about now.

So I stood up, grabbed the stack of papers, and dropped them in the trash.

Then I stepped out into the living room, preparing to tell Noah about James. He was going to be so upset.

The two of them were still sitting there at the table with a deck of what appeared to be Tarot cards.

Aurora drew a card from the deck and gasped.

"The Ten of Swords..." she said dramatically, holding the card out to Noah. "Heaven help us... This can mean many things... None of them good... Deep and painful loss... Insidious deception from trusted loved ones... Tumultuous endings to cherished relationships..."

"Oh, enough already." I snatched the card from Noah to take a look. It pictured a young man on the ground with ten swords in his back, bleeding out — alone in the woods.

"Cheerful as ever," I grumbled, flicking the card back onto the table.

Aurora looked up at Noah with bulging eyes and trembling lips.

"Sweet boy... I sense a devastating betrayal in your future."

End of Patient File: ⊅BridgeToAurora

Our Sixth Date ♡

The storm was over just in time for our next date, which was really good timing, because this was going to be the best date of all!

We were standing deep in the jungle by a waterfall, and Doc was eyeing me suspiciously.

"What are we doing here?" he asked.

I gave him a big smile. "Are you ready to get splashed?"

His eyes went wide. "Noah, I didn't bring a bathing suit!"

"Just go in your boxers!" I said, stripping off my shirt and jeans.

He looked terrified, which was definitely not the reaction I was hoping for.

"I'll just — I'll keep my clothes on."

I swallowed nervously as we stepped closer to the waterfall. This wasn't exactly how I imagined the night going, but that was okay! Doc could still have a good time getting soaking wet... in his collared shirt and jeans.

I stepped under first and laughed as the fresh, warm water splattered off my head.

"Come on!" I held out my hand.

Doc hesitated, but eventually took my hand and stepped under with me. I was disappointed to see that he looked stressed out as the water splashed all around us.

I pulled him into a tight hug, hoping that might help to relax him. He stiffly reciprocated.

As we stood there together under the rushing water — with my half-naked body wrapped around his fully clothed torso — I couldn't help but notice that it was a pretty accurate representation of us as a couple.

Doc was a hard shell to crack. He was very kind to me — most of the time — but it seemed like he was always holding back a part of himself. Still, I really felt he could open his heart to me if I kept showing him how much I cared.

Before I could continue over-thinking everything, Doc suddenly pulled me closer and looked into my eyes.

My heart raced. What was happening?

And then he leaned in, closed his eyes, and kissed me.

It was the most incredible kiss of my life — like a million fireworks exploding inside of me. Everything was just like I remembered from his rooftop. Soft, tender lips. Gentle, caring touch.

I tightened my arms around him and returned his kiss, pouring every ounce of my heart into it. Even if I was too scared to say the words out loud, I wanted him to know just how much I... loved him.

We continued like that for a long time, making up for every date we didn't kiss.

And finally, we both looked up and smiled at each other, our cheeks bright pink in the moonlight.

Doc let out a big breath. "I've been wanting to do that for a long time."

"Me too!" I said.

We took each other's hands and sat down under a calmer part of the waterfall, so a gentle stream massaged our backs and necks.

I wished we could stay like this forever.

"Noah, there's something I need to tell you."

Anxiety flooded my core. Every time we were happy, something bad seemed to happen.

"Y — Yeah?"

Doc bit his lip. "Do you remember James?"

"Of course!" I said. "The boy from the beach."

"Right," said Doc. "Um, I recently learned that... That his mother died."

My heart sank. "No!"

"I know," said Doc, bowing his head. "It's horrible. And she was his only relative."

"So what's going to happen to him!"

"Well, his mother's will sort of... listed... us... as his guardians."

I raised my eyebrows. "You and me?"

"Yeah." He nodded. "And obviously we're not ready to like, adopt a child or anything. But I was thinking maybe we could at least take turns caring for him, so he doesn't have to go into the foster system?"

"Of course!" I said. It wasn't even a question in my mind. "Of course I will."

"Really?" said Doc. "Okay, that's great. I was also thinking I should probably take a step back from therapy for a while, since my patient files aren't exactly child friendly."

"That makes sense!" I said, unable to contain my relief. Over the years, Doc's practice had become increasingly dangerous — to the point where I wasn't really sure I could be his assistant anymore. I had been wrestling with the idea of resigning after Aurora's warning, but now I didn't have to!

I couldn't believe Doc was willing to leave behind his

practice to take care of a child. This entire night was just solidifying my love for him. Without his dangerous patients, it was starting to feel like we could actually have a happy ending together.

"You know…" I cuddled up close to him. "This all fits really well with the sixth key!"

"Really?" said Doc. "What's that?"

I kissed him again and then looked into his eyes.

"To do something selfless."

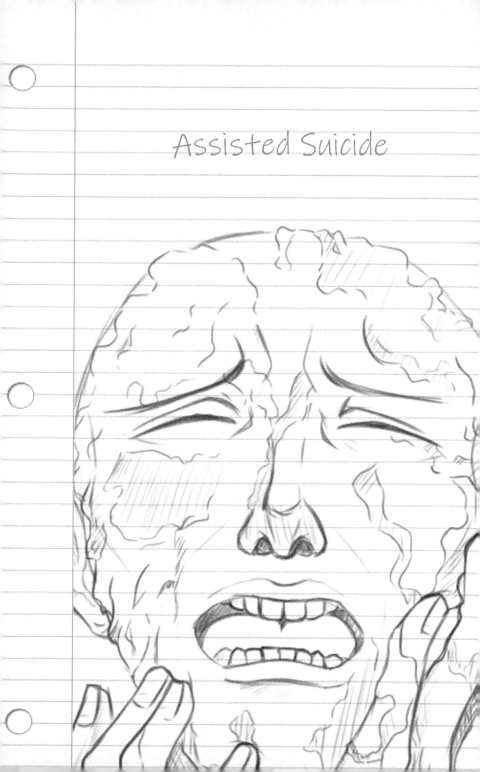

Assisted Suicide

PART ONE

"You ready, doc?"

Noah peeked his head through the door, wearing a polka-dot bathing suit and a pair of Kierra's oversized heart-shaped sunglasses.

"Almost," I said. "I'll meet you at the beach."

"Okay!" He grinned. "Don't forget sunscreen!"

I nodded and waited for the sound of his footsteps to fade away.

The last day on the island looked like it was going to be blue skies and sunshine. The storm had cleared, and there were no patients left to talk with. No threats, no worries, no problems. Just one final pool party to bring everyone together.

But Kierra had gone off the radar again this morning, and I just couldn't shake the feeling that she was up to something.

So yes, I did plan to join Noah at the beach. But first, I was going to make a quick detour.

Hurrying out of the room, I veered off from the beach trail and headed north.

To Linus Solomon's fortress.

I know, I know... I already asked Bruce to check it out. But I'm a control freak, and I had to investigate for myself.

Kierra's story yesterday didn't make any sense. Why was she

out for a walk in the middle of a storm? And how did she end up a mile away from our rooms?

If Noah would just tell me why she was here, I wouldn't have to snoop. But his blind trust in her was not reassuring to me in the slightest.

Fifteen minutes passed, and I found myself standing once again at the front door of Linus's fortress.

I took a deep breath and entered the code: 74291

First came the familiar sound of compressed air, and then the locks clicked.

I stepped inside and left the door open behind me, to avoid getting locked in this creepy place.

Looking around, it felt even creepier than last time.

Without Linus and my friends, it just felt like some sort of dark, sterile prison.

I looked around the kitchen, opening every drawer in search of a clue I didn't know existed. Just... something to explain Kierra's behavior.

Everything seemed to be exactly as we left it.

Except...

Across the way, I saw something red pooling around the office door. Was that... blood?

Heart racing, I grabbed a knife from the counter and hurried up to the door.

"Hello?" I said shakily. "I have a weapon!"

No answer.

I turned the doorknob and jumped in, knife raised.

"HELP!"

I gasped as Bruce grabbed my leg and coughed blood all over my feet.

"Holy shit," I said, dropping the knife as I bent down to help him. "What happened?"

He tried to talk, but all I heard was a gurgling choking noise.

That was when I realized his throat had been slit.

"Jesus fucking Christ..." I whispered. I scrambled to rip off my t-shirt and tie it around his neck.

The blood kept coming.

The wound was too deep.

"Bruce, I'm going to call for help," I said. "But you need to tell me what happened. Can you nod or shake your head instead of speaking?"

He started choking more blood.

"Hang in there, Bruce…"

I reached for my phone, but he smacked my hand away.

Tears were streaming freely down his cheeks, which was an extremely unsettling sight for a man like Bruce. He looked like a man who knew he was about to die.

He fumbled in his pocket and handed me a pair of keys.

"K — Kierra…" He sputtered, spraying blood all over my face. "The pool party."

"What about her?" I asked, leaning closer. "What's happening at the pool?"

His final word was delivered with pure terror in his eyes. "Hurry."

PART TWO

I sprinted through the jungle trails, desperately trying to get ahold of the security team. Why wasn't anybody answering their goddamn phones?

When I finally made it to the pool, I was panting and soaked in sweat.

But looking around at the scene in front of me, I didn't see anything wrong.

A massive wave pool. Hundreds of people laughing and floating in the water with drinks in their hands. Trop house blasting with the sun beating down.

"Doc, there you are!"

I spun around to see Noah, who was staring at my torso.

"Noah, where is Kierra?"

He stared for another second and then looked up, cheeks pink.

"Oh! Uh — She went to go check on something."

"Check on what?" I said urgently. "Noah, something really bad is about to happen here. Bruce is dead."

"What?" His eyes went wide.

"Did you see where she went?"

He pointed to the other side of the pool, where a firetruck was slowly backing toward the pool.

Kierra.

"Jesus Christ…" I breathed. "EVERYONE GET OUT OF THE POOL!"

"Doc, what are you—"

"Get out of here, Noah!" I broke into a sprint and screamed

at the swimmers. "OUT OF THE POOL, NOW!"

Nobody was listening. Nobody cared.

I had to get to that firetruck.

"DEVASTATING BETRAYAL!"

Out of nowhere, Aurora Borealis appeared and ran toward me, arms flailing in the sky.

"NOT NOW, AURORA!" I shouted, trying to run around her

Every step I took, she stepped in the way. "INSIDIOUS DECEPTION!"

"MOVE!" I shoved her aside and she fell to the concrete with a cry.

"Yo! You gonna push an old lady?" A strong young man jumped up from the pool and pinned me to the ground.

"Let me go!" I struggled. "Someone's about to attack this pool."

"Bro, you're the only one attacking!"

I looked up and saw the firetruck begin to spray a stream of water into the pool. Everyone started to cheer.

But within moments, the cheers turned into screams.

"OH MY GOD!"

"IT BURNS!"

"ACID!"

My eyes widened as I realized what was happening. Mass panic ensued as swimmers scrambled to get out of the pool. Hundreds of people, stuck in a giant vat of water turning to acid.

The security team scrambled around the firetruck and attempted to open the door to no avail.

Then, without warning, Noah sprinted past me and did something I will never understand.

As the security team slammed at the door with crowbars, Noah's eyes darted between the pool of screaming swimmers and the stream of acid coming from the firetruck.

And that's when he grabbed a nearby table, brandished it like a shield, and jumped in front of the spray.

"NOAH, NO!"

I desperately wrestled the man on top of me as I watched

acid splatter from the table all over Noah's arm and torso. It wasn't hitting the people in the pool anymore, but it was burning him alive.

My heart lurched as Noah screamed in agony.

It was a horrible sound that I've never heard come from any human.

PART THREE

The idiot on top of me finally realized what was happening and let me go.

"NOAH!" I begged, sprinting toward him. "PLEASE STOP!"

He heard me, but I saw him shake his head as his clothes seared onto his skin.

And then, as if things couldn't get any worse, I realized that Kierra was running up behind him. What the hell? I thought she was driving the firetruck.

"NOAH, WATCH OUT!" I shouted.

She punched him in the balls — hard. He fell to the ground and then I was surprised to see her kick his body out of the spray.

Acid now freely showered the people in the pool again. I'll admit that I felt a horrible selfish relief that Noah was out of harm's way, despite hundreds now burning alive.

But then to my disbelief, Kierra stepped in front of the stream of acid — where Noah had been blocking before.

"What the hell?" I breathed out loud.

In stark contrast to Noah, Kierra did not scream or look terrified. She just stood in eerie silence as acid melted the skin from her body and face. I had to look away from her.

Why was she doing this?

People were screaming and crying as they scrambled out of the pool. I noticed many of them were covered in red burns, but nothing like the horror that was happening to Kierra.

I finally made it to the firetruck and grabbed the key Bruce had given me.

"OUT OF THE WAY!" I shouted at the security team.

They moved and I unlocked the door to see a familiar face at the wheel.

What the fuck?

Rocky looked down at me with a grin. "Enjoying the party?"

I jumped into the firetruck and wrestled him out of the seat, yanking him down to the concrete as I punched him in the face as hard as I could.

"SOMEONE TURN OFF THE FUCKING SPRAY."

The security team rushed into the truck behind me and finally the stream of acid fizzled out.

I continued punching Rocky until I was confident he wouldn't escape.

Then I hurried over to Noah and Kierra.

Both of them were sprawled out on the ground, unmoving.

"She's ready to see you now," said the doctor. "I have to warn you, ninety-eight percent of her skin is burned."

I nodded and followed him into the hospital room. We were back home now, and Kierra had finally awoken from her medically induced coma.

When I saw her in bed, I had to stop myself from gasping.

Her entire face was red and black. Her hair was gone, replaced by raw patches of burnt skin.

A ventilator puffed at her side, along with a million other wires and devices.

"I'll give you some privacy," said the doctor, taking his leave.

"Kierra," I said gently, sitting down next to her. "The doctors said you wanted to talk with me?"

I was almost positive that the doctors had made a mistake. Why in the world would I be the first person she wanted to see?

But she nodded.

"How's Noah?" she whispered.

"He's already up and walking," I said. "His left arm and side got the worst of it. The rest of him is fine."

She closed her eyes and gave a small smile. "Good."

"Kierra — how — why?"

I didn't even know where to begin. I had so many questions

for her.

"We don't have much time, Dr. Harper," she said. "So I'm going to get straight to the point. I need you to disconnect that little machine over there."

She tilted her head toward the ventilator.

"Why?" I raised my eyebrows. "Is it causing you discomfort? Let me call a doctor."

"No!" she hissed. "My entire fucking *body* is causing me discomfort. Unplug that thing and let me die in peace."

I looked at her in horror. "I'm not doing that!"

"You've got to be kidding me..." she groaned in pain. "I'm giving you a chance to end my life. Isn't this like... a dream come true for you?"

"I never wanted you dead!" I protested.

"Great," she said. "I ask you for one fucking favor and you can't even—"

"Why me?" I asked. "Why would you ask me to do that?"

"Because you're the only one with the moral compass to do what I'm asking."

"How is this a moral issue?" I asked.

"I am in *agony*," she breathed. "Even with the painkillers, every second is pure torture. Like a thousand burning hot knives piercing through my flesh."

"We can up your pain meds!" I suggested. "The pain will eventually get better."

She let out a raspy laugh. "Even after the pain, what kind of life do I have? Look at me."

"You look fine!"

"Fuck you," she said. "Don't fucking lie to me, Dr. Harper. I expect that shit from everyone else, but not from you. I look like Freddy Kreuger's asshole."

"Kierra... You can still live a long and happy life—"

"Stop." She closed her eyes. "I'm asking you to pull the plug. Please do not make me beg. Please do not humiliate me further."

I took a deep breath and looked at the ventilator.

"I'll *consider* what you're asking," I said. "If you tell me what happened on the island."

She peered at me through a pair of burnt eyelids.

"Deal. What do you want to know?"

Everything. I wanted to know everything.

"How did you know Rocky was still alive?" I asked. "They said he used Tetrodotoxin to fake his own death, but how did you know that?"

"I didn't," she said. "I thought maybe he was carrying Zach's sperm samples on him when he died, so I broke into the room where they put his body bag."

"You were trying to exonerate Zach?"

"Yeah," she said. "But his body bag was filled with a bunch of pillows."

"Why didn't you tell me!"

"Because you were a fucking asshole to me the entire trip," she said. "You never trusted a thing I said."

I went quiet and bit my lip.

"Anyway, that's why I was out in the rain. I searched the entire island for him while everyone was cooped up inside. My search came up empty, until I got to Linus's germ box."

"You found Rocky inside?"

"I couldn't go inside," she said. "I didn't have the code. But I saw a light come on — right when you guys showed up. So I figured I would check back when the weather cleared."

"You were there the morning of the attack?"

"Yeah, that's when I found Bruce," she said. "All fucked up and bloody. He told me that Rocky had attacked him and ranted about getting vengeance for the acid attack — making the influencers ugly on the outside like they were on the inside. And something about a firetruck at the pool. So I ran back to the pool party—"

"You left Bruce?"

"I thought he was dead," said Kierra, as if it should have been obvious. "He seemed dead."

"But... When I found him on the ground, he said *your* name — not Rocky's!"

"He was probably telling you to find me at the pool, you dolt." She let out a painful sounding cough. "So anyway... I got to the firetruck, but I was too late. Rocky had already locked himself inside. And the rest is history... As you know."

"I just don't get it," I said. "Why did you jump in front of the acid like that?"

She let out another laugh. "Fucking sixth key."

I raised my eyebrows. "What?"

"You know Noah and his happy keys, right?" she said. "I'm trying to follow them. The sixth one is to do something selfless. So when I saw the brainless hero clamoring to save the world by jumping in front of acid, I thought... No, you're not gonna out-selfless me, you little shit."

I frowned. "You're following Noah's keys?"

"Yeah, as you can see, I'm a shining example of the program's success."

"Have the keys actually helped with your... condition?"

She glowered. We both knew that I was talking about sociopathy.

"I'm not really in the mood to be psychoanalyzed—"

"No, I'm just curious," I said. "From a completely non-psychological perspective."

She snorted. "The keys don't fucking work. Look at me. People like you and me, we're broken. Forever."

"Kierra, you sacrificed yourself to save others," I said gently. "You wouldn't have done that a year ago."

"I did it for selfish reasons," she said. "Even when I'm supposed to be selfless, I'm selfish."

"How could that possibly be selfish?"

She let out a hollow laugh. "Because I wanted the keys to *fix* me."

"What do you mean, fix you?"

She closed her eyes as the ventilator compressed and expanded.

"I'm sick of waking up every day with that boredom gnawing away at my soul. I'm sick of being unable to reciprocate the things people say they feel for me — all I can do is mirror and mimic them. I'm sick of knowing I should be angry or sad about my past, but being unable to feel those things even when I try my hardest. It's like I've been banished from my own body, and no fucking *key* is going to let me back in."

I listened to her words in disbelief. Noah had made more progress with her in a few months than I had after an entire year of keeping her locked in my garage.

"Kierra, that's actually incredibly hopeful."

"Oh, spare me—"

"No, I'm serious," I said. "Your healing journey is only just beginning. You have so much to look forward to! Maybe your body hasn't caught up yet, but your mind and spirit are already transforming. Kierra, your character is defined by your *actions*, and your actions saved hundreds of people on that island."

She made a retching sound. "Okay. Therapy time is over. I answered all of your questions. Time to hold up your end of the bargain."

"Wait," I said. "I have one more question."

She sighed. "What?"

"Noah kept saying he trusted you to be on the island, but he wouldn't tell me why. He said there was some secret you didn't want me to know…?"

Kierra laughed. "Captain chatterbox seriously kept it quiet the whole trip? Wow. I owe Zach a hundred bucks."

"What's the secret?" I pressed.

"No," she said. "Fuck off."

"Fine," I said, standing up. "I guess I'll just leave you with Zach and Noah. I'm sure either of those golden boys will help you commit suicide."

She glared at me as I walked away.

"Stop."

I turned around. "Yes?"

"Don't make a big deal of this," she said. "And — don't *ever* mention it again."

"Deal," I said, coming back to her side.

"Back during your trial…" She took a shallow breath, like the words pained her to speak. "I testified for your defense. Against the cult — against my parents."

I nearly fell over. "You… What?"

"I said don't make a big deal!"

"Kierra," I whispered. "I don't know what to say. I had no idea — thank you so much."

"No, don't you dare get sentimental with me," she said. "I didn't do it for you. I did it for Zach and Noah."

"Well, either way, I appreciate it."

"Well, either way, you still suck."

I smiled at the ground, happy to dismiss so many of my false assumptions about Kierra.

"KIERRA!"

Noah came bursting through the door and dove toward the bed for a hug.

"Noah, don't!" I yanked him back before he landed. "She has third degree burns all over her body. Hugs don't feel good."

"Oh, right!" he said, kneeling down next to her. "Kierra how are you feeling?"

She stared at him. "Never better."

"That's great!" he said. "Incredible job with the sixth key. Are you ready to start working on the seventh and final key?"

Kierra's eyes widened into a murderous glare, and the heart rate monitor began to spike.

"Noah," I said hurriedly. "Why don't we let Kierra rest for a few minutes."

"Sure thing!" He joined me at the foot of the bed. "Are you excited to pick up James this afternoon?"

As planned, Noah and I were going to take turns with James while we figured out a long-term plan for him.

"Can't wait," I said. "What time does the cab get here?"

"Two hours!" he said. "I'm just finishing up my hospital paperwork now. Jeez, medical bills sure are expensive. Isn't it kind of weird that people have to pay money for getting hurt? There should be some sort of system to help people cover their hospital bills when they get sick."

"Commie," Kierra grunted from the coach.

A few minutes later, Zach joined us in the room and greeted Kierra.

"Glad to see you up. We missed you."

She raised her eyebrows. "They let you go, then?"

"Yeah," he said with a grin. "They found my... samples in his firetruck — along with six other vials. A lot of innocent people will be exonerated."

"Wow, it's an Un-Canceled success story," she said. "We should donate to Rocky's non-profit."

Zach laughed and turned to me.

"Listen, Elliot," he said. "I know you've got a lot going on, but I just got a call from this abandoned mental institution in Transylvania. Guy claimed to be an escaped patient. He said they're experimenting on humans with some sort of permanent anti-depressant."

My heart started to race with a familiar excitement. "What? Do you think there's anything to it?"

"I do," he said. "I've been digging into things, and there's an insane amount of activity from the electric and gas lines. That place is *not* abandoned."

"Are you going to check things out?" I asked.

"Yes," he said. "The plane leaves in a few hours. Are you in?"

I raised my eyebrows. "Am in *in?*"

"Well, yeah!" he said. "I need you, Elliot. This is kind of your area of expertise."

I turned to Noah, who had been listening to our entire conversation.

"Noah, would you be able to take care of James for a bit?"

Zach walked over to the door. "You guys talk it out, and let me know what you decide. I need to finalize travel arrangements as soon as possible."

He exited the room, leaving us alone at the foot of Kierra's bed.

"Well?" I asked.

Noah didn't respond. He was just staring at me, and I noticed his eyes were beginning to water.

"What?" I frowned. "Are you — are you crying?"

He continued looking at me, eyes burning red. Then he shouted:

"What is WRONG with you?"

I jumped, taken aback. I don't think I had ever heard him yell in my life.

"Excuse me?"

Tears fell freely down his cheeks now. He pointed at his burnt arm. Then he pointed at Kierra.

"Look at us!" he said. "You want to do this *again?*"

"I just want to help!"

"Oh my god..." Noah breathed. "I am such an idiot. I thought all of this would change things—"

"Change what?" I demanded.

"Your practice!" he said. "I thought seeing your friends get hurt might make you reconsider jumping into scary situations. But you're — you're already excited for more. It's like you have some sort of death wish!"

"Noah, therapy is my *job.*"

"This isn't therapy!" he cried. "Therapy doesn't leave behind a trail of bodies—"

"I can't help that!"

"Yes you can!" he protested. "You can choose *not* to fly away and investigate this scary mental hospital."

"Then who will help them?"

"THE POLICE!" he shouted again, throwing his arms in the air. "That's who you're *supposed* to call when people are in danger."

"Who are you to tell me how to do my own goddamn job?"

"We're in a *relationship!*" said Noah. "You can't just run around putting your life in danger anymore. There are people who care and worry about you."

"How is this a relationship?" I hissed, the pressure inside of me building up. "We went on six dates."

He looked devastated, which only made me angrier for some reason.

"We—" he stammered. "We're about to pick up a child that we committed our hearts and homes to."

"So you're forcing me to choose between us and my job?"

"I'm not forcing anything!"

"Yes, you are." I crossed my arms. "This is an ultimatum, and I refuse to take part in it."

Noah looked at me, cheeks blotchy and wet.

"No, Doc." He shook his head. "An ultimatum is when you force someone else to make a choice. I'm not forcing you to do anything. I'm making my own choice."

He swallowed and turned away.

"What is that supposed to mean?" I demanded.

He turned back one last time with a sniffle and looked into my eyes. "Goodbye, Doc."

Then he walked out the door without another word.

"Hey!" I called, trailing after him. "Where are you going?"

Before I made it to the hallway, I heard a dark chuckle from the bed.

"WHAT?" I spun around, not in the mood for Kierra's bullshit.

"Oh my god." She started laughing harder. "You suck."

"How do I suck?"

"Oh, you suck!" She was laughing so hard that she started choking. "You suck so much!"

I stormed over to her bed. "What the fuck are you talking about?"

"You've been..." She let out a few shaky breaths to stop laughing. "You've been gifted a happy ending — Hallmark style. Loving boyfriend. Sweet kid. Body not burnt to a crisp. And you feel like the *victim!*"

"He was being unfair!"

"Please stop making me laugh — it's fucking painful!" she wheezed. "Even *I* know that relationships require compromise, and I'm a fucking sociopath!"

"I'm TRYING!" I said, growing frustrated. "I've never dated anyone before."

Kierra smirked. "It bothers you, doesn't it?"

"What bothers me?"

"How open and free he is with his heart," she said. "All that love and affection... It's like a constant reminder of your own inability to connect."

I looked down uncomfortably. "You have no idea what you're talking about."

"I was *married* to him, Dr. Harper," she said. "I fucked with his head because I couldn't stand how much happier he was than me."

"It's not like he's perfect," I said defensively. "He's obviously codependent, and—"

She interrupted me with another laugh.

"He *was* codependent," she corrected me. "Not anymore. Codependents don't walk away from a toxic piece of shit — like he just did to you. And that's the whole reason your little dynamic with him is falling apart at the seams. Because he's *not* codependent anymore. You thought you found a punching bag who would never leave you, no matter how nasty you got—"

"I'm not nasty!"

"Yes you are!" said Kierra. "You're a fucking asshole to everyone. You're rude, you're impatient, you're judgmental. Not to mention, you're an earless freak with a burnt dick. And all of this brings me back to my original thesis statement, which is... You suck."

I crossed my arms. "Well — Well he started this whole fight. And he left, which makes him even worse than me."

"Oh my god, GET HELP!" she howled. "Seriously, talk to someone! You are a fucking disaster."

I shook my head. She was wrong. Noah was being completely unreasonable. I wasn't going to sabotage my career just to make him happy. If he really cared about me, he wouldn't put me in that kind of position in the first place.

As my mind raced with a million imaginary arguments, Zach peeked his head through the door and asked me a simple question — one that would soon come to define the rest of my life.

"Elliot, are you coming?"

The End

A Few Years Later

A Few Years Later

Sometimes I wonder...
Would I be happier if I made a different choice?
Would I still be friendless, alone, and afraid?
The choices we make define our reality. I made mine, and now I have to live with it.

I was stuck here in this godforsaken mental asylum — miles from civilization — locked in a straightjacket next to the other human experiments.

"Please," I begged The Pharmacist. "Do what you want to me. Just... Take the letter from my shoe."

The Pharmacist glared at me for a moment and removed my shoe, reaching in to find a folded envelope.

"It's already addressed and stamped," I pleaded. "Please... Just send it."

I needed Noah to know the truth.

The Pharmacist took one more look at the letter, rolled his eyes, and tossed it in the trash.

"No!" My voice shouted, and my heart screamed.

How had it come to this?

I was completely alone in this world, and I had no one to blame but myself.

Zach never talked to me again after he learned what I did to Kierra. And Noah... Oh god, how could I have fucked things up so badly with Noah?

As The Pharmacist approached me with the syringe, I prepared for the dose. The world's first permanent anti-depressant. With one side effect: losing the ability to love and feel emotions.

Forever.

But maybe it was a blessing. My heart was already damaged

beyond repair. I lost Noah. Nothing else mattered anymore.

I closed my eyes and felt the sting in my arm.

Moments later, everything faded to numbness.

It was a strange feeling — a foggy haze where I could still remember Noah and all of our adventures together, but I felt... Nothing. No sadness. No joy.

Just an infinite emptiness in my heart.

Goodbye, Noah.

Goodbye.

Noah put down the laptop and gave me a strange look.

"Well?" I asked impatiently.

"It's..." He raised his eyebrows. "Well, it's a bit bleak, isn't it?"

"I'm a horror author," I said, growing more self-conscious by the second. "Horror doesn't have happy endings."

"But we *are* happy!"

"If we live happily ever after in the book, I can't exactly keep publishing more sequels."

Noah nodded and gave me a forced smile. "You're the boss!"

"I can tell you hate it," I said irritably, snatching the laptop back. "I'll change it."

"Don't change it on my account." Noah leaned over and gave me a kiss on the forehead. "People like your depressing books, sweetie."

"Ugh, don't call me sweetie." I brushed him away. "I'll change it."

"You'll have to do it later," said Noah, walking toward the door. "They're almost here!"

"Is it already three?" I muttered out loud.

Noah nodded and left the room, leaving me alone with the manuscript illuminated on my laptop screen.

After going to therapy — as a patient — I left behind my own practice and decided to become an author. Zach introduced me to his publisher, and the stories are loosely based off of my patient files. I write under a pseudonym, of course, and I've changed all patient names and identifying details. It's certainly a more peaceful career path than my years as a therapist, and the royalties are enough to ensure Noah gets the life he deserves.

I took one last read through the epilogue and sighed. Noah was probably right. This *was* bleak. He was better at story-telling than me — that's why I always consulted him for creative input.

So I followed his advice and went in for the kill.

Select All + Delete

The truth was a better story anyway.

"James, can you clear off the table when you have a moment? They're almost here."

The dining room table was covered with painting supplies — brushes, canvases, and dozens of bright colors. James and Noah had been working on an art project all afternoon.

"Sorry, dad!" James scrambled to clean everything up. "We got super distracted and lost track of time. No idea what happened to my alarm. I swear I set the volume on loud. I wonder if my phone is broken. Or wait, hmm... Maybe I never set an alarm."

"No worries." I gave him an encouraging smile.

I couldn't believe he was already in high school. It seemed like just yesterday that we finalized the adoption with a terrified kid who barely spoke. Now he never stopped talking. He definitely got that from Noah.

He was also a gifted artist, spending most his free time creating these beautiful paintings. He didn't get that from either of us. But Noah always loved painting with him — even if their creations were a bit... different.

On James's easel, there was an incredibly detailed painting of our home in the mountains, with a sunset that cast vibrant colors across the peaks.

Noah had attempted to paint the same thing, except with

gumdrop mountains, heart-shaped clouds, and sunglasses on the sun.

"Here!" James handed his painting to me.

I raised my eyebrows. "You don't want to take it to school?"

"No, it's for you!" he said.

I smiled and took the painting. "Thank you so much. I love it."

"Wait!" Noah ran into the room and grabbed his painting from the easel. "This is for you too!"

I took his painting in my other hand. As I looked at them both standing there in front of me, all I could do was shake my head in quiet disbelief.

Noah tilted his head. "What?"

"Nothing…" I said.

But as I hung their paintings on the dining room wall, I felt something strange in my heart.

———————————— // ————————————

"They're here!"

Our two rescue dogs ran up to the front door, barking like mad. Right behind them was our extremely annoying cat, Aurora, who started running in circles and meowing dramatically.

James stepped over the animal circus and opened the door.

"Welcome, welcome…" I said, reaching out to take their bags.

"Nice to see you, asswipe." Kierra punched me in the arm.

"Ow!" I massaged the spot. "And watch your language in front of James."

"Oh, I'm sorry." She ruffled James's hair. "Nice to see you, buttwipe."

"Auntie K!" James stifled a laugh.

"Look at this place!" Zach patted the dogs and looked around in awe. "Guess the books are treating you well?"

James ran up and hugged him. "Uncle Z!"

"Speaking of which… When are you going to tell us your

pseudonym?" said Kierra. "I don't trust you writing about us. You probably make yourself look noble and tolerable, but we all know Auntie K is the real hero of the story."

I rolled my eyes. "Come on out to the deck, guys."

We made our way outside to my favorite part of this house.

"Holy..."

Even Kierra was speechless as she ran up to the wooden railing and looked out across the sweeping mountain range. Then she glanced to her side and did a double take.

"Is that — Is that a fucking *hot tub* on your mountain deck?"

"Language, Kierra!"

"You didn't tell us to bring bathing suits!" she pouted. "What's the matter, didn't want to see my crispy skin in a bikini?"

"Auntie K, it was in the invitation!" said James.

She paused for a moment and then lunged at him. "Now listen here, you little shit."

He giggled uncontrollably as she chased him around the deck.

Zach stepped up next to me at the railing and put his arm around my shoulder.

"I'm so happy for you, buddy."

I smiled. "Thanks, Zach."

Over the next few hours, we devoured Noah's vegan feast, played fetch with the dogs (and Aurora), and told stories about the old days.

"Ever wonder why you have to eat this vegetable shit?" said Kierra to James as she chewed loudly. "Ask your dad about the special hamburgers we ate on the island."

"Kierra!" said Zach. "Not at dinner!"

"That was the quiet patient!" Noah chimed in. "Shawn, right? I really liked him!"

"My personal favorite was the surprise plague," said Zach with a grin.

James's eyes went wide. "Surprise plague?"

"Oh, you're in for a treat..." Zach leaned forward. "It all started with a squirt of hand sanitizer..."

As Zach told the story, I sat back in the Adirondack chair and just listened as everyone gasped, laughed, and bickered about the little details.

And then I felt it again.

That strange feeling in my heart.

What *was* that?

"James is doing homework," I said, stepping down the stairs after everyone left. "Want to watch the sunset from the tub?"

Noah's face lit up. "Definitely!"

Without a second thought, he ripped off his shirt and dropped his pants, standing there in his boxers in the middle of the kitchen.

I stared at him for a second. Then I laughed and did the same thing.

We shoved each other playfully and ran out to the deck.

As we settled into the warm bubbles, we looked out across the world. A brilliant sunset splashed the mountain peaks with gold, just like James's painting.

As the colors faded to shadows, we talked, we laughed, and we kissed. Time seemed to stand perfectly still, but twilight soon arrived to share its own kind of magic... Mountains silhouetted against the night sky. Constellations dancing in the moonlight. An eternal universe of stories waiting to be told.

And here we were, living our own little story, in our own little corner of the universe.

I took another glance at Noah, who was smiling at me while he applied a bubble beard to his neck.

And then — in that moment — it finally clicked.

I realized why my heart felt strange.

For the first time in my life, there was an absence of discomfort.

And without the discomfort, all that remained was...

Peace.

Thank you so much for finishing the series. Your support and enthusiasm has made me the happiest writer in the world.

This is the end of Dr. Harper and Noah's story, but there is one last surprise for the readers.

Sign up on my website to claim your spot:

www.DrHarperTherapy.com

@DrHarperTherapy

/r/Dr_Harper

If you enjoyed the book, please consider leaving a review on Amazon to help others discover my files.

Made in the USA
Middletown, DE
21 July 2020